Groundwood Books is grateful for the opportunity to share stories and make books on the Traditional Territory of many Nations, including the Anishinabeg, the Wendat and the Haudenosaunee. It is also the Treaty Lands of the Mississaugas of the Credit. In partnership with Indigenous writers, illustrators, editors and translators, we commit to publishing stories that reflect the experiences of Indigenous Peoples. For more about our work and values, visit us at groundwoodbooks.com.

**WARNING: EXPLICIT CONTENT.
(WHAT WERE YOU EXPECTING?)**

EDITED BY **KARINE GLORIEUX**
TRANSLATED BY **SHELLEY TANAKA**

Groundwood Books
House of Anansi Press
Toronto / Berkeley

Published in English in Canada and the USA in 2025 by Groundwood Books
Text copyright © 2022 by Éditions de la Bagnole, Montreal, Canada
Translation copyright © 2025 by Shelley Tanaka
Originally published in French (Canada) as *Ma première fois: Recueil de nouvelles sexu*

All rights reserved. No part of this publication may be reproduced, stored in a retrieval system or transmitted, in any form or by any means, without the prior written consent of the publisher or a license from The Canadian Copyright Licensing Agency (Access Copyright). For an Access Copyright license, visit www.accesscopyright.ca or call toll free to 1-800-893-5777.

Groundwood Books / House of Anansi Press
groundwoodbooks.com

We gratefully acknowledge for their financial support of our publishing program the Canada Council for the Arts, the Ontario Arts Council and the Government of Canada.

Library and Archives Canada Cataloguing in Publication
Title: First times : short stories about sex / edited by Karine Glorieux ; translated by Shelley Tanaka.
Other titles: Ma première fois (2022). English
Names: Glorieux, Karine, editor. | Tanaka, Shelley, translator.
Description: Translation of: Ma première fois. | In English, translated from the French.
Identifiers: Canadiana (print) 20240413089 | Canadiana (ebook) 20240416546 | ISBN 9781779460349 (softcover) | ISBN 9781779460356 (EPUB)
Subjects: LCSH: Teenagers—Sexual behavior—Fiction. | CSH: Short stories, Canadian (French)—Québec (Province)—Translations into English. | LCGFT: Short stories.
Classification: LCC PS8323.E75 M3713 2025 | DDC jC843/.01083538—dc23

Cover and interior illustrations by Simone Duchesne
Edited by Karine Glorieux

Printed and bound in Canada

Though these stories are inspired in part by real individuals, they are works of fiction. All resemblance to real events is pure coincidence.

Groundwood Books is a Global Certified Accessible™ (GCA by Benetech) publisher. An ebook version of this book that meets stringent accessibility standards is available to students and readers with print disabilities.

Groundwood Books is committed to protecting our natural environment. This book is made of material from well-managed FSC®-certified forests, recycled materials, and other controlled sources.

Contents

Foreword
    Karine Glorieux   9
Hugo Nguyen
    Edith Chouinard   11
Rolling a One
    Jérémie Larouche   31
Always Ready
    Alexandra Larochelle   45
This Ain't Your Grandpa's Pipe
    Nicolas Michon   61
Leap into the Unknown
    Vanessa Duchel   89
The Great Fat Bird Migration
    Olivier Simard   102
My ~~First~~ Time
    Laurence Beaudoin-Masse   117
My Chouchounette, My Faith and Me
    Schelby Jean-Baptiste   130
The Sad Story of My Virginity
    Pierre-Yves Villeneuve   148

Foreword

When it comes to sexual relationships, there is something exciting about the idea of the "first time."

Exciting, and scary.

It feels like you've been waiting for this moment for a long time. Something that will only happen once, so you must be ready. Because you think you have to get it just right.

A first time has to be like in the movies! Close-ups of smiling faces, a connection, a communion — even a *symbiosis* between two people, with music playing in the background — pleasure, happiness, *ecstasy*!

Whoa.

It's pretty stressful, a first time.

Or not.

Maybe we should get rid of this pressure, which also suggests that the first time is the one you will never forget — the baseline for all the others to come.

Because the truth is that there is not just one single first time. There are first *times*.

First times with yourself, first times exploring a certain part of your own body or somebody else's. Amazing first times, confusing first times, fascinating first times.

Sometimes disappointing ones.

And that's okay, because sexuality isn't discovered in a single moment. It reveals itself bit by bit, over time.

The internet makes it look simple. Just learn the positions, the words to say, the moves to make. But no one tells you that bodies will make weird noises, that they will smell different, that fluids will leak out. That you will be embarrassed to find yourself naked, both physically and metaphorically.

And, yes, it is all embarrassing at first. Some people say it always will be. Being comfortable with being naked — you can't learn that from a guide.

But we can start talking about it.

Karine Glorieux

Hugo Nguyen
by Edith Chouinard

My hair is dripping onto my still-damp skin. Slowly but surely, my face is hydrating under a layer of day cream, and I reek of green tea deodorant, which I think I've applied at least three times.

I'm looking at myself naked in the big mirror hanging on the back of my bedroom door.

I look closely, check myself out.

I love my arms. I've always loved them. They aren't too dangly.

I can't say the same about my thighs. They rub together so much that I never need to worry about freezing to death. My thighs could start a fire anywhere, anytime.

My eyes linger on my round hips, then on my plump little belly, where a few stray hairs keep popping up like weeds. Grrrr.

After a few plucks with the tweezers, I carry on with my examination. My right breast is bigger than the left, which drives me nuts. Sometimes I want to give them names, just to make them seem more likable ... Like Mario and Luigi, Batman and Robin, or Elsa and Anna. But I don't. I'd rather wait until I get a boyfriend. Naming your breasts seems like the kind of thing that should be done with another person. I wouldn't want to have to introduce them to him. "So here's the thing. This is Mario, and that one's Luigi." Ugh.

I admire my freshly trimmed pubes. I'm glad I finally got up the nerve to make an appointment with the beautician. She did a nice landscaping job. It's beautiful, clean.

I turn around to look at my butt. Everything is as it should be. No pimples or any unsightly rash to report.

Overall, I'm not too unhappy with what I see in the mirror: Nadine, a seventeen-year-old girl, maybe a bit soft in spots but with impeccable body hygiene!

I put on my Wonder Woman panties. I read somewhere that girls have more confidence when they wear sexy or matching underwear ... Me, I need my blue boy briefs with my favorite superhero logo.

I strike a pose. It was my aunt Nina who taught me how to do this. Stand up nice and straight, feet slightly apart, fists on hips, chin lifted, and look out into the distance like you want to save the world ...

There's no better way to give yourself a little jolt of energy.

And tonight I need to feel brave.

Tonight I'm going to sleep with Hugo Nguyen.

Tonight I'm going to have sex for the first time.

*

My friend Axelle throws the best parties. It was in her basement that I drank alcohol for the first time — this blue stuff that tasted like Mr. Freeze, yuck. It was in her backyard that I kissed a guy for the first time — why did you have to move so far away, Jayden? And it was in her pool that a guy touched my boobs for the first time—that same guy. I miss you, Jayden!

I walk across the living room arm in arm with Axelle. There are already quite a few people here, and music echoes through the big house.

I scan the room to see if Hugo Nguyen is here.

Negative.

Hugo Nguyen is the cousin of a friend of a friend. He goes to another school, lives in another city. We don't see each other that often. Just often enough.

"He must not be here yet," my friend says in my ear.

"We should have stayed in the kitchen. I would have had a better view from there."

What if he didn't come? But he even texted to tell me we'd see each other here.

I take out my phone to read his text for the hundredth time. My heart beats faster. I'm pretty sure my armpits are already sweating. Shit!

"You okay, Nad?"

"Yeah, yeah."

"Are you sure? You know, there's still time to change your mind …"

"Don't worry. I'm ready. I know it's going to be awkward. The first time everything always goes wrong. It's just normal to want to get it over with as fast as possible, right?"

"Uh … no."

"Hmph."

"Anyway, just remember you can stop the whole thing anytime you want. No means no."

At that very moment, Hugo Nguyen walks in the other end of the living room.

I give my friend a big smile. "And yes means yes!"

Hugo is quietly greeting his friends who are gathered in a corner.

I take a deep yoga breath and force myself to count to ten.

One … two … three … four …

Too long! I rush in his direction.

When I finally catch his attention, I feel him light up a bit. He smiles at me in a reassuring way. He knows what's going to happen tonight too …

I move closer and completely barge into their conversation.

"Hi!"

"Hey, Nadine. You know Alex and Jay?"

"No, sorry." I take Hugo by the hand. "You coming?"

I drag him with me while Alex and Jay start to whistle, and we head upstairs, followed by cheers and the grunts of rutting animals. I feel my cheeks redden, but I pretend not to hear.

Come on, Nadine, have some guts!

At the top of the stairs, Hugo follows me to the last door at the end of the hall. It's the guest room.

I turn the handle ... but it stays stuck.

It's locked!

What the ...?

I try to open it again, but it won't budge.

Hugo raises his eyebrows.

Plan B. Axelle's room is right next door. I turn the handle ... and stumble across a couple making out on the bed!

"Hey! The door!"

I close it fast.

Okay, so Axelle's room is taken. Maybe that's just as well. I don't know if I want to lose my virginity underneath her giant BTS poster. That's a lot of people watching ...

I lean against the wall of the hallway, and Hugo fixes his eyes on mine.

"I'm happy to see you," he says.

"Me too."

Hugo Nguyen is so handsome. His hair is black as night, short on the sides, long on top. He has slanted eyes, beautiful golden skin and perfectly sloped shoulders.

Honestly, I never thought I'd be hot for shoulders, but that's what's happened. Big time.

He gently presses his lips to mine.

"I've thought about you a lot since the last time."

"Me too."

I kiss him back. Full on the mouth.

His hands slide down my neck, then onto my back and down to my butt.

The surprise of it makes me jump, and I push him lightly on the shoulders. His beautiful shoulders ...

I suddenly hear Axelle's voice in my head. "You're so not ready! What's the big rush? Why don't you wait until you have a boyfriend you love and who loves you too?"

Oh, shut up, Axelle! I'm just a little nervous, that's all. I'm ready, I know it. I did my research! And I had an endless discussion with my mother, and another with my aunt Nina. I got condoms and lube at the pharmacy — without even buying other stuff to disguise them!

I'm *so* ready.

"Follow me," I say quickly, to cover up the awkward moment.

I take a few steps and open another door. This is Axelle's parents' bedroom.

When we go in, the light reveals a large room decorated Japanese style. I close the door carefully. I drop my bag on the floor and lightly kick my sandals into a corner one at a time.

I take Hugo's face in my hands and kiss him again and again. I push him toward the bed while he pulls me there. Like a tango that's out of sync and a bit ... sweaty.

Finally, we fall on the ultra-big, ultra-low bed. Not exactly a smooth landing! As my back absorbs the shock, I burst out laughing. Okay, so it's a bit of a nervous laugh, but at the same time, this is pretty hilarious. I feel like I've just fallen from the second floor.

But Hugo doesn't find it so funny. He smiles, then wrinkles his eyebrows.

"Are you okay?"

"Yes, absolutely. Sorry."

I stop laughing. I take a deep breath, then I pull his face toward mine to find his lips again. It's getting hotter and hotter ...

I put my hands under his T-shirt to take it off. His head doesn't even get caught in the neck! I don't want to jump to conclusions, but, seriously, I've got this.

I stroke his chest, then his perfect shoulders ... I lift up my head to kiss him again, but smack him right in the face, which is moving toward my cleavage.

"Ouch ..." Hugo breathes, raising his hand to his jaw.

"Sorry!"

He carefully brings his lips to my neck and the top of my breasts. I decided to wear my black bra for the occasion — the one that pushes my breasts all the way up. It's not the most comfy, and I can't wait to take it off. But at the same time ... um, I don't know anymore. Elsa and Anna might be a bit shyer than I thought.

Hugo starts to stroke them through my T-shirt. Good. I'll wait to see where this leads ...

He keeps kissing me, moving up my neck to my ear. He starts to suck on my earlobe like it's a Chupa Chups lollipop, and it sounds a bit disgusting.

It feels like it's never going to end. At this point, I decide to take things in hand, and when I say "things," I'm talking about his crotch.

I can feel his erection through his jeans. Check.

This isn't the first time I've felt it. It was right there last time we kissed for a long time ... at the ice cream place.

So I'm not surprised or panicked, but now I have to do something about it, and it's stressing me out a bit.

Just as my fingers move toward his jeans button, Hugo finally lets go of my ear.

Yay! I feel his hands slipping under my skirt, which he lifts up with no problem.

Whoa.

All of a sudden, I no longer want to be proactive. I let things play out ... and try to relax.

The atmosphere in Axelle's parents' room is set up to help me — it's like being in a miniature Zen garden. All that's missing is the sand and the little rake.

But I'm as stiff as a board.

Then suddenly everything stops. Hugo raises his head and looks at me.

"Uh ..."

What? What? What?

Did I miss a stray hair? The really long kind with a little spiral at the end? Is it my cellulite? Because I don't really feel like explaining to him that it's perfectly normal for girls my age to have it.

"Your underwear ..."

My underwear? What?

"Is that ... Wonder Woman?"

Sorry, dude, if you were expecting a black lace G-string.

He lowers his head again. His nose brushes against my thigh as he whispers, "It's cute."

Oh, he's killing me!

I feel like we're getting closer to the jackpot, so I slide off my Wonder panties myself. I'm trembling, but I don't think Hugo has noticed. He lies down next to me and puts his hand where only my own hand has ever gone before. His finger wriggles its way in, and I quickly feel myself melt like a Popsicle, running everywhere ...

Then, just when I'm finally forgetting where I am, he brings me thumping back to earth.

"You've never gone all the way, huh?"

"Uh ... is that what it seems like to you?"

He shrugs. I'm waiting for him to say more, hoping to understand what he's getting at, but he doesn't say anything else.

That's what I love about Hugo. He's a super good communicator — *not*.

That's when it hits me. This is my first time. I might bleed ... on Axelle's parents' white bedspread! I can't believe I didn't think about this. Yet I know it's normal to bleed a little if my hymen tears, blah, blah, blah.

I hear his fly open with a quick *zip!* and I decide to be the kind of girl who doesn't bleed. Surely there are more of them than we think.

I breathe deeply again.

"You okay?"

"Oh, yeah. I have condoms in my bag. Do you want to take care of it, or do you want ..."

"Nadine, relax."

He gives my bent knee a quick kiss before going to get my bag. I want to sit up and watch him, but I keep my eyes fixed on the ceiling.

I hear everything — the package tearing, the squish of the latex, Hugo's breath speeding up ...

In no time, he's back on top of me.

I stop breathing.

"Okay?" asks Hugo.

"Yes."

"You're beautiful."

"Thanks."

I'm trying to lighten the mood, but obviously, I don't know how!

"Have you done all this before?" I ask him.

"Yes."

"Often?"

"Yes."

That's not the impression I'm getting. He's moving around all over the place, and as soon as his penis seems ready to make its entrance, it bumps into a closed door.

"You okay?"

"Yeah ... hang on a sec ..."

I breathe. I inflate my stomach to the max. Then I exhale loudly from my lungs.

I do that twice. Three times.

Hugo's face starts to tense up, and his arms begin to shake.

"You can lie on top of me, you know. I can take it."

I arch my back to get into a new position as he finally stops doing the plank.

At the same time his penis returns to its position at the starting gate. It's nice ... but why doesn't he keep going? I don't get it! It should be easy enough putting a round rod in a round hole. It is *literally* child's play.

"Are you sure you want to?"

"Yes!"

"Okay ... because I don't really know what to do. Can I push harder?"

"Um, yes."

"I don't want to hurt you."

"No, no. Go ahead. It's fine."

I. AM. READY.

But what I feel then, as his penis struggles to make its way inside me, is a terrible pain. It lasts just a few seconds, but it's enough to make me let out a little cry.

Hugo immediately pulls back.

"Listen," he says. "I think we should do something else."

I sit up and pull down my skirt. I run my hand through my hair and grab a few loose bobby pins.

"Wait, I ... why do we need to do something else?"

I look straight at him searching for an explanation, but all I can see in his eyes is the black of his irises.

"Well, it's not working."

It's not working.

"Do you maybe want to ..."

He sits on the bed and looks down at his penis, still at attention. I watch it standing there, so sturdy inside its little raincoat, and I feel a weight slowly pushing down on my chest.

It's not working.

I feel tears stinging my eyes.

"Okay, worst idea ever," he says, grabbing his jeans. "Forget it."

With the back of my hand, I swipe at the tears running down my cheeks. My throat is tight. Even if I wanted to say something, the words would stay stuck there.

"It's okay. Really. I'm just going to the bathroom. Okay?"

Hugo puts on his T-shirt and gives me one last look before disappearing into the adjoining bathroom.

It's not working.

I'm ... paralyzed. The weight gets heavier and heavier. I stare down at my undies on the floor but see nothing.

I hear the water running in the bathroom. I have about two seconds before Hugo comes back. I have to pull myself together! I pull on my panties, grab my bag and my sandals, and rush out of the room. I run down the stairs two at a time.

On the ground floor the party is in full swing and the noise hits me like a Mack truck. The heavy beat. The crowd. It's suffocating. I lower my head and choke back a sob as I look for the front door. Have they moved it? I need to get out of here!!!

Like, now!

*

Sitting in my little blue car, I'm already feeling better. I lock the doors and turn on the radio. This is the only thing that lets me pretend I'm somewhere else. I wipe my tears, blow my nose, breathe ...

It's not working.

I grab my phone and search *First time having sex penis won't go in.*

I find a lot of information, and basically it says that I have no reason to worry, that it happens, that the muscles of your vagina sometimes decide for you ...

But the thing is, this doesn't reassure me at all. I'm the one who decides if, where, when, how and who with. I'm the boss, not my vagina!

I search some more and find that it can be a chronic condition—vaginismus, dyspareunia, pain during intercourse ...

How come I've never heard about this before?

Frustrated, I put my phone in my bag. My keys brush against my lap, and I notice the Loki key chain my aunt Nina gave me. I can't wait to talk to her. Surely she'll be more reassuring than Google ...

I sigh as I fall back against my seat and close my eyes to try to regain my composure. But all I can think about is Hugo's face asking for a blow job because the entrance to my vagina is blocked. Grrr!

I hear a dull noise. I open my eyes and see Axelle's shocked face through the windshield.

"No!" she screams at the top of her lungs.

My friend is lying across the hood of the car, arms stretched out on each side.

"You can't leave now! I won't let Hugo Nguyen spoil your evening!"

I'm laughing so hard that I'm having trouble waving at her to get off the car. I turn on the windshield wipers — which I think is hilarious — and she's so surprised that she loses her grip and disappears down the front of the car.

She resurfaces on the passenger side, where she keeps yelling through the window.

"I want you to stay! I love you!"

She tries to open the door at the same time that I'm trying to unlock it. Of course it won't open. We go back and forth like that for a few seconds until she finally flops into the passenger seat.

Her breath reeks of alcohol.

"What are you doing? You can't leave!"

"I know."

That shuts her up.

"I can't leave because, look, there's a car parked right behind me."

Weirdly, I am ready to lose my virginity in Axelle's parents' bed, but not willing to ruin their flower beds by running over them with my car.

Axelle looks out the front and back windows, then blushes when she sees that I am well and truly stuck here, and that she was freaking out for nothing.

I pull her close and put my arm around her.

"I love you too."

We spend a minute or two like this, without moving.

"How did it go?" she asks, leaving her head on my shoulder.

"Bad."

She sits up, looking upset, but I won't let her say a word.

"I don't want to talk about it right now." I don't have the strength to listen to one of her I-told-you-so speeches. Not tonight.

"Tomorrow, okay?"

"Okay ... but first let's take your mind off it. Come back inside."

"No, I know I won't have fun. And I don't want to spoil yours."

"Come on! Fuck Hugo Nguyen."

"Oh, I wish!"

I laugh, but it's not that funny.

"You go back inside," I tell her. "I'm going to wait here quietly until it's clear."

"Are you sure? It could be a long and boring wait. Whose car is it?"

"Don't know."

"There can't be that many girls who drive a white car with a mini sombrero hanging from the rearview mirror."

"True."

"I'm going to find out whose car it is and tell them to move it!"

"If you want, but you don't have to —"

I don't have time to finish my sentence before Axelle opens her door to go on her mission.

"Hey, Axelle."

"What?"

"Thanks."

She gives me a look that makes me feel better. I'm

smiling as I watch her stumble off toward the house. Something tells me that she's already forgotten what she's supposed to do.

But whatever. I'm willing to wait. I turn off the radio and sit in the quiet. Then I take out my phone again to open a Duolingo lesson. Nothing like learning Spanish to avoid thinking about Hugo ...

Tap! Tap! Tap!

... who is now tapping on the passenger window with his finger.

"Can I talk to you?"

I'm torn. Are Axelle's parents' flower beds really that beautiful? Maybe they could do with a little plowing after all!

"Please," he adds.

I'm afraid to let him in, but ... it's my car. My territory. It's okay.

I reach over to open the car door. He slips in next to me.

"Why did you leave like that?"

"Why do you think?"

He looks away, bites his lip. It's the first time I've seen him do that.

He turns to me again.

"Axelle said you were out here. She's looking for someone who loves Mexican food. I don't quite get why but ..."

I let out a little laugh.

"Are you okay? Do you want to talk about it? It might

be a good idea to ... I don't know, things have always been cool between us, and then now, it's like ... No?"

"What?"

Hugo laughs, too. He runs his hand through his black hair, which flops back down over his forehead.

"Yeah, sorry, I wasn't clear. Basically, I didn't want you to think that ... well, I didn't want you to think that I didn't want to ... I don't know ... try again?"

"Really?"

"Of course."

"You know, I was afraid that ... but ... that it was ... I wasn't prepared for what ..."

I remember the feeling of his penis bumping against a closed door, and I have even more questions than I did before. I wish I had enough courage to ask him.

So, Hugo, what did I do wrong? Is it my pelvis? Do I need to move around more? Like to the front or back? Should we have used lube? Do you think it's the condom? Maybe we need to talk about it some more ... well, what do you think?

Argh ... I can already see him making a fast getaway, leaving behind a cloud of dust like in the cartoons. Even worse, I'm sure he'll laugh at me, tell all his friends about it ... Rumors will start spreading—I have a serious problem, I'm frigid, not fuckable ...

Maybe it's like naming your breasts. Maybe it's the sort of discussion you can only have with your boyfriend, or with someone you know well and trust.

Hugo Nguyen looks at me. For once it's not particularly

intense or drawn out. It's like a little butterfly landing nervously on the end of my nose.

"I think you're really cool, Nadine."

He smiles and shrugs, as if he's afraid of what I'm going to say.

I open my mouth, but nothing comes out.

He looks around nervously.

"Why did you drive to the biggest party of the year? You didn't want to drink or smoke? Hey, I don't even know, actually ... do you smoke weed?"

"Sometimes. But tonight I wanted to be in full control. I had plans ..."

"Yeah, me too."

Finally we both laugh at the same time, at the same joke. It's weirdly refreshing!

"You know, Hugo, I think this is, like, the longest conversation you and I have ever had."

"Yeah," he says, running his hand through his hair again.

I don't know what to say anymore but I carry on. "I think you're really cool, too. But I think I'd like to get to know you better before ... we go any further."

"Uh ... okay," he says, and he smiles.

Hugo Nguyen takes my hand and slides his fingers between mine. Even though his tongue has already made several trips around my mouth, I get the feeling that I'm sharing a super intimate moment with him.

"Do you want to go home?" he asks.

"Yes, but I have to wait until the end of the party." With my free hand, I wave at the car parked behind me. "I'm stuck here."

"Not if I move my car, you're not," he says, grinning as he dangles his keys in front of my face.

Rolling a One
Jérémie Larouche

Hi, I'm Jérémie. I'm a thirty-eight-year-old cis man. I would say that I'm bisexual, and I use he/him pronouns.

I'm a comedian, author, TV host, teacher at the National School of Comedy. And, most important, of course, I'm an expert on ketchup chips.

I love to make people laugh. Especially when I'm embarrassed. It's my defense mechanism.

For example, I have a Lovecraftian fear of giving blood. So I try to make the nurses laugh as much as possible ...

Not recommended, to have a person laughing while they're sticking a needle in your vein. It hurts!

I consider myself a nerd, a geek. To give you an

example, I created a show where I sum up the entire *Star Wars* plot using cardboard puppets.

I know what you're thinking. And you're right. I have no sex life! (I also created a show called *Harry Paper and the Cardboard Parody*—just saying.)

I just want you to catch my vibe before we start. I have full-on ADHD, and since I write like I talk, watch out as you read. This is going to be a bit all over the place, like one of those inflatable tube men at a used car dealer.

SECOND-CHANCE CREDIT! EVERYTHING MUST GO! BIG SALE UNDER THE BIGTOP! OWNER HAS LOST HIS MIND!

Happy reading, my friends!

*

When I was asked to write for this collection, I tried to think back to my *real* first time. My first sexual moment with another person, if you will (or first sessual moment, if you're someone who can't pronounce the word properly).

Things are going to get pretty dark, but ... all will end well, I promise.

At least, I think it will.

Even so, just in case, spoiler alert.

Trigger warning: unsolicited kissing.

So, basically, when I was twelve years old and my girlfriend kissed me at the pool, I wasn't that into it.

I'm going to go back to the summer I was twelve and a half, in 1996, when I was kissed on the mouth for the first time — in all my splendor as a weak-mustached adolescent who didn't shower every day.

Why do I consider my first kiss to be my "first time"? Because I don't think a sexual relationship is defined just by penetration. That's so heteronormative and so ... so 1996.

My first kiss was the first time I realized that sexual desire had to be at play — on both sides of a kiss.

Let's travel back in time to another century — another millennium!

Suddenly, a car appears — a DeLorean DMC-12 turned into a time machine with its flashing lights and electronic beeps. Cue the theme from Alan Silvestri's *Back to the Future* soundtrack.

(Oh, yeah ... let's do it — find the soundtrack on Spotify and follow along.)

Cue the *Back to the Future* theme music by Alan Silvestri!

(But not the main theme ... you know the one that goes "pa-papapa-pa-pa-paaa"? Not that one! Go to the soundtrack of the second film, *Back to the Future Part II*, the "Burn the Book" track by John Debney and Alan Silvestri performed by the Royal Scottish National Orchestra. (I told you I was a nerd (so why not a third parenthesis?).)!)

We've set the temporal convector to July 17, 1996,

Montreal, Canada, at the outdoor pool in St-Georges Park in Pointe-aux-Trembles. Wheels burning tracks in the sky at 88 miles per hour!!!

    Great Scott!!!

*

Cue "Quit Playing Games (With My Heart)" by the Backstreet Boys. (Yeah, I know, it's a mood killer, but those guys were in their prime in 1996!)

    I remember this song playing at the pool, in the lifeguard room, even though it was released later in October 1996 ... I know I'm a nerd who likes precision, but memories can be subjective, okay? (hahaha) Imagine the scene with the palette and image quality of a VHS cassette — those were the days!

    I'm twelve years old, wearing fluorescent swim trunks with Bart Simpson saying, "Eat my shorts." It's hot, the sweat is running down my three new armpit hairs. These hairs fill me with a strange mix of pride and embarrassment. You know, like when you fart so loud that it makes the cat jump? You're proud, but ... you can't really brag about it.

    I'm with friends at a picnic table just outside the pool fence, and the corner of my mouth is stinging because, well, I just cut it on the plastic of a Mr. Freeze.

    Yeah, a relatively rare injury. The boo-boo heals quickly, but not the wound to one's pride ...

If life was a game of *Dungeons & Dragons*, cutting the corner of my mouth with a Mr. Freeze would be like the wound the Dungeon Master inflicts on you if you roll a one. For the information of all you Muggles or non-nerds, rolling a one with a twenty-sided die from *Dungeons & Dragons* is what we would call an *epic fail*, a fatal blunder for your character.

Rolling a one is pretty much what happens to my mouth, but there's a good reason for it. I wanted to see how deep I could shove the Mr. Freeze down my throat before the gag reflex set in.

Not so deep, as it turns out!

Are you getting the picture?

A kid with a rattail practically makes himself vomit on a Mr. Freeze on a dare from his friends.

At least it's a nice white Mr. Freeze. Cream soda, the best Mr. Freeze flavor! Forget about blue! No ... give it a try and you'll change your mind. White is the best flavor. Red has no personality. Blue? You think you're better than everyone else. Orange? Might as well drink a Gatorade. As for purple — what? No, not purple. Who likes purple? Refresh yourself with something that tastes like a kid's fever medicine?

WHITE IT IS!

Fact is, I clumsily spear my soft palate with the sharp corners of my "Missafizz," as that person with the bad diction would say. To avoid throwing up, I quickly pull it out and the plastic cuts the left corner of my lip. It stings like a papercut, and after five minutes of silence, when I open my mouth to say something, the cut reopens and it stings all over again.

Not cool.

It's these two simultaneous humiliations — a gag reflex and a papercut — that have my friends laughing at me.

The song on the radio changes — "Good Enough" by Dodgy.

Well, it's not good enough for me! I'm in pain. This is taking a long time. It's hot.

And I can't wait for my girlfriend to arrive. She's supposed to join us here.

A friend asks me if I've finally kissed her, Sandra Bullock.

(Yeah, I'm not going to tell you the girl's real name. I'm going to call her Sandra Bullock because back then, ever since the movie *Speed* came out in 1994, I had a *total* fantasy about Sandra Bullock — the Kleenex industry was making a fortune off me. I wanted to be like Keanu Reeves, and I still do, in fact.)

I manage to avoid the subject of whether Sandra Bullock and I have already kissed. A yellow car goes by.

"Yellow car!" I yell. "Punch buggy no punch back!"

That was a time when you punched someone in the shoulder every time you saw a yellow car. But you didn't cry if you got hit, because that would mean you were a faggot. Right, 1996.

"Lovefool" by The Cardigans comes on.

They ask me the question again. I blush. I don't know what to say. Things start spinning in my head. In fact, I know I don't want to answer because I know what I don't want to tell them.

The truth. No.

They'll start to call me a virgin.

In 1996, this is the worst insult. A guy who hasn't got the game to get a woman. Remember that my male role models were guys like Harrison Ford. In *Star Wars*, *Blade Runner* or *Indiana Jones* he always kisses women by force, like they're something to be conquered. He knows what she wants! And blah, blah ...

Girls are super complicated ...

Sandra Bullock and I have been going out for a couple of months, but we don't broadcast it too much because we don't want to be hassled about it. And she doesn't go to the same school as me. We know each other from Scouts ...

Yeah. I'm in Scouts. I've got everything it takes to be the coolest guy in the school, with my three new mini armpit hairs, my girlfriend I haven't kissed yet, and who "goes to another school" — which basically makes people assume that she doesn't exist, and that she's a lie made up to hide the fact that I'm a loser or, worse, *homosexual*!!! (*Sigh* this *is* Pointe-aux Trembles, my friends!)

I love my Sandra Bullock. The reason I haven't kissed her yet is because I don't know how. Also, she has braces and I'm afraid of cutting myself.

No, wait! She has braces in 1996! It's like having a bear trap in your mouth!

Well, looking back, it's no big deal, but I was afraid. Don't judge me. I'm twelve and a half, and I cut my mouth easily back then.

I'm afraid to kiss her and then suddenly find out I'm not good at it ... it's not something you can practice ... or maybe you can ... I don't know.

But at night I dream about it when I'm, you know, helping the Kleenex industry make a fortune.

Don't judge me, I'm only twelve!

I'm afraid of kissing her and rolling a one. Like getting a surprise erection and she sees it, or worse, feels it.

I'm twelve years old and I constantly have to be careful about what I'm thinking. Surprise erections are a nightmare. Especially at the pool. In a bathing suit, you can't hide it with a T-shirt or too-big pants. If you have the misfortune of making eye contact with the beautiful lifeguard, QUICK! HIDE YOUR FELLA!

It's harsh.

Obviously my penis is going to betray me when I'm with Sandra Bullock, and I've always been told to wait until I get married. In my family, sex is not so much a taboo subject, but it is awkward. We never talk about it. So, yeah ... I guess it is taboo. Ha ha.

I realize that "Ready or Not" by the Fugees is playing on the radio ...

MY GOD! I've been lost in my thoughts for a whole

song??? How long have I been spinning around in my own head? (At that time I hadn't yet been diagnosed with ADHD. That doesn't happen until I'm thirty-four.)

I try to reply with my teeth full of blood, but it's too late. They know.

"No, I haven't kissed her yet."

They laugh. They treat me like I'm pathetic.

Then guess what? I drift off into my own thoughts, head in the clouds like a good ADHDer, to dream about the perfect kiss, right? And I get an erection!

And at *this very moment*, Sandra Bullock arrives.

What. Are. The. Odds.

Back then, we didn't have the famous facepalm meme of Captain Jean-Luc Picard in *Star Trek: TNG*, but it would go riiiiiiiight here!

She's giving me a weird look. I know what they're planning. My friends are preparing me for the inevitable by asking the question. They know. I feel betrayed.

Sandra Bullock has decided that it's going to happen today. She is going to make a man out of me.

A few days ago I refused to kiss her and she cried. She took this as a rejection. Like I didn't really love her. Like I found her repulsive. And, well, maybe I did say, "Ew!" But it wasn't about her! If she only knew how much I've dreamed of touching her breasts. Of kissing her. Of melting at the smell of her Wild Blackberry Dans un Jardin perfume—a scent that, strangely, still turns me on even now.

My friends grab me by my arms.

"You're going to kiss me if you love me," Sandra says. I'm trying to run for my life. I've rolled a one. EPIC FAIL.

They're playing Céline Dion's "It's All Coming Back to Me Now" on the radio.

Here I am pressed with my back to the fence, held by four "friends" (note the quotation marks).

Just before the end of Céline's song, Sandra Bullock presses her lips against mine.

So many emotions are bouncing around in my head, my heart, the butterflies in my stomach.

It finally happened.

I'm relieved. It's done. Finally. I'VE LOST MY KISSING VIRGINITY. I KISSED A GIRL. I AM NOT QUEER. People will stop bugging me.

Is the rite of passage done? The love gods appeased? Are they up in the clouds giving us a thumbs-up? Happy now?

But I'm not happy. I'm mad. I have two reactions at the same time. My head is saying, "Okay, you're not dead, it's over." But my eyes are filled with tears. My throat is tight.

What just happened?

I am, however, freed from my former state of oral virginity.

I feel like telling everyone to fuck off. They're laughing. I want to evaporate, disappear, never exist again. I am ashamed. I am shaking more than the first time I rode the Boomerang at La Ronde.

People in the pool are looking at me. In my mind, a hundred million of them are laughing at me. Even the kid in a diaper in the wading pool seems to be giving me a thumbs-down.

I spit again and again to get rid of what tastes like a venom of blood, white Mr. Freeze and Sandra Bullock's Lypsyl.

It's like I've made up for some bad thing I've done to her ... repaired some harm, like I've made amends for some insult, like I'm finally a real man ... as if NOW we're a real couple ...

But I've just been attacked.

My first kiss was an assault.

Against the fence of the St-Georges swimming pool, with everyone watching. With my friends laughing and yelling, "You're a real man now, Larouche!"

It's only today, at the age of thirty-eight, that I understand what happened.

I see myself again leaning over my bike, struggling to get my lock open so I can get the fuck out of there because my eyes are full of water, and when you lean over with eyes full of water, it just gets worse. Everything gets blurry and every small wave of tears makes your eyes sting.

I cry all the way home on the bike path.

But when I get there, I can't tell my mother. I need to calm down. Breathe. I can't go home like this.

What am I going to say? I'm bawling because a girl kissed me! Really?

My mother's going to say, "Girls who chase boys are just cheap bimbos."

I pedal as fast as I can to try to outrace the thoughts in my head ... but my brain has stronger legs than me and can pedal faster: Sandra Bullock is a nice girl. It's my fault. I'm an asshole. I don't know how to say I like you. A fucking asshole. I made her cry. I should have just kissed her. Just done fucked her, why not ...? Show that I like her, that I want her. Why isn't it that simple? Now she thinks I don't like her. She must be crying with her friend who already doesn't like me much ... She's going to tell Sandra Bullock to dump me. She's going to dump me. What are they going to say? Fuck, it's someone I know ... he didn't see me, phew. Christ, almost home and I'm still crying. Breathe. Okay. Okay. Breathe. How come life is so hard? Life is cruel, like Zeus hurling down chocolate éclair lightning bolts at diabetics! Christ, I just want to die. My mother's going to think I'm gay! Fuck. Now I'm stuck dealing with this myself. Fuck, fuck, fuck ...

Now we come back to the present in the time machine. There is a big silence in the car for the whole ride.

*

You okay?

I'm okay.

I don't know how much time I spent riding around on

my bike before going home. I don't even remember how it ended. I kept going out with Sandra Bullock.

I've always thought the whole thing was my fault. I even apologized.

Because back in 1996, there was no such thing as sexual assault if you were in a relationship. A kiss isn't an aggression, right? A girl can't assault a guy, right? (Unless you're a professional wrestler. HAHAHAHAHAHAHA, YOU GUYS ARE HILARIOUS!!!!)

It took the accusations of the #MeToo movement for me to realize that I was a victim. Fuck.

My first kiss was an assault.

Something I'd always seen as a deserved humiliation — a consequence of my own actions, an initiation. That I was the one who was getting it all wrong, who wasn't mature enough, who wasn't grateful for the experience.

I don't blame Sandra Bullock. In fact, I don't blame anyone in this story from 1996. It was the mentality of the time.

We went out for at least a year, me and Sandra Bullock. I kissed her many more times after that. We would play hide-and-seek with her little brother. I would look and on purpose never find him ... ha ha. Instead I'd find Sandra Bullock and we would kiss — necking for long minutes with drool running down our chins because we weren't very good at it. And her braces never cut me. I would stroke her body and she would stroke mine. I was happy. The scent of her Wild Blackberry Dans un Jardin perfume.

But it's clear that this incident affected my life. No one was responsible except for the ideology of things like the patriarchy, toxic masculinity, homophobia or the fact that we were frightened by the values of religious conservatives. I could blame ignorance, the fact that instead of talking about things, instead of educating us, things were just forbidden. I could blame the taboos, or why not blame capitalism?!

At the time, I blamed myself. For being weak. For not being enough of a man.

I've often asked myself why I've always felt the need to make people around me laugh. Being funny isn't a job for me, it's a necessity! (BTW, my favorite laugh is that crazy kind when you're laughing and crying at the same time. My God, that feels good!!!)

Why do I need to make people laugh? Maybe it's a defense mechanism, a way I've developed to be in control. So that in the end, and once and for all, *I* decide how and why the people around me are going to laugh. It's okay if they laugh at me. But *I* am going to be the one to make you laugh ...

I don't know. Maybe I've never known.

But if my need to make people laugh is linked to my first kiss, fine. I have succeeded, at least subconsciously, in transforming that into something good, something funny.

The 1996 radio is playing "You Learn" by Alanis Morissette, and it's beautiful.

Always Ready
Alexandra Larochelle

My head was buried in my math notebook, my brain boiling. *Sin, cos* and *tan* were taking up all the space and threatening to come out my ears.

But I absolutely had to finish my homework, or else my parents wouldn't let me go to the party that I had to be at in … just two hours.

The big mirror near my desk reminded me just how not ready I was for the party. Getting control of the shaggy mess known as my hair was going to be harder than trigonometry. Unless I just ended up tearing out all my hair from not being able to understand anything, in which case, I was already off to a good start.

There were three little taps at my bedroom door, which was ajar.

"Can I come in?" said my father's voice.

"Yes, Dad."

His head appeared around the doorframe.

"You okay, sweetie?"

"Ugh ... I suck at math."

My father shrugged with a sorry smile.

"At least you don't have to do it for much longer," he said cheerfully. "Just two short months until the end of school!"

I liked that he didn't try to contradict me, like a lot of other parents would have, saying things like, "Don't say that, of course you're fantastic at math!" Blah, blah, blah. I was terrible at math, and my father wouldn't try to convince me otherwise, even though he always congratulated me when I improved and always pointed out other areas where I excelled. He was always straight with me, and I loved that.

He came in and handed me a plastic bag from the pharmacy.

"I have something for you."

I grabbed the bag, curious, and looked inside to find ... a box of condoms.

"They have spermicide in them," he explained before I could say anything. "Which means you have even more protection against pregnancy."

I felt a vague smile freeze on my lips, as I tried to figure out whether this was a joke.

"Um ... okay? For ... why?"

"Well, you're sixteen now, you've got a new boyfriend, and I wouldn't want you having sex without protection just because you don't have condoms on you. By the way, I want you to put some in your bag."

I was mortified. Talking to my parents about sex had always been easy and natural, except this was the first time I'd been subjected to an intervention quite so ... obvious.

"I ... okay, thanks. I will." I stared at him, waiting for him to leave my room, but he just stood there.

"Right now," he ordered.

Oh my God. I felt like I was eight years old (except my parents were not giving me condoms when I was eight). I sighed and got up to drop a handful of them in my purse.

"You know, Frédéric and I haven't even talked about having sex. You don't have to worry about that right now."

"I'm not worried," my father said. "And I know what it's like to be your age. Not talking about it doesn't mean it won't happen soon. This is all he's waiting for."

I frowned.

"Why would you say that?"

"Because a guy is always ready. That's just the way we're wired. It will be up to you to set the limits, because for him, guaranteed that the second you open that door even slightly, he's gonna be ready to jump in with both feet. Now, go back and study if you want to be able to go out and have fun soon!"

*

The music in Simon's basement carried to the end of the block. The sounds of beer bottles clinking, yelling and laughing were woven together like a kind of happy symphony.

But at the end of the hall, on the other side of the storage room door, the atmosphere was completely different.

Over the rumbling of a giant freezer, sounds of kissing and sighing broke through the silence. Fred had me leaning against the wall so he could press against me, and his lips ran down my neck in a way that was making me lose my mind.

We'd only been together for a month and a half, but it felt like we'd known each other forever. Plus, we didn't go to the same school, which meant every moment we had together, every kiss and touch, was really special.

While my boyfriend squeezed my butt, I felt a familiar heat spread through my belly, right down to my groin. My heart was beating fast, and I sank into the sweet tingly feeling that became more and more intense every time I was with him.

I kissed his neck.

"I want you, Fred," I murmured in his ear.

It was the first time I'd said these words, and just hearing myself say them had a weird effect, like it increased my desire for him.

He looked at me with his big gentle eyes and gave me a smile that was both loving and mischievous.

"I want you, too."

I smiled back at him.

"Oh, really?"

"Really and truly," he nodded.

I laughed a bit nervously.

"So ... what do we do about that?"

He interlaced his fingers with mine and laughed.

"I can think of a few things. But ... not here."

Doing it for the first time between Simon's parents' jars of pickles and frozen chicken nuggets didn't exactly appeal to me, either.

Except there was one catch. Frédéric had a little brother, a little sister and two parents. In other words, his house was never empty.

As for me, my parents were literally at home *all the time*.

Which meant that if we wanted a bit of privacy, one of us would have to get rid of our family for a few hours.

"I could probably ask my parents to leave us alone next Saturday. What do you think?"

Fred pretended to think about it. "Hmm, I think that sounds like a good idea."

"Really?"

"Yup."

I felt his erection against my leg, and then he went back to kissing me passionately.

*

"Hey, love!" Fred's voice came over the phone. "Have a good day?"

"Yup, not too bad. You?"

The truth is, it felt like this Thursday would never end, just like every other day that week. It felt like every minute went on forever, and Saturday would never come. Only two more sleeps until the end of our virginity.

We'd talked on the phone every night since Simon's party, but we hadn't raised the question of our momentous first time, which was fast approaching. I think we were a bit shy and also afraid someone in our family would overhear us talking about sex (especially his ten-year-old sister, who always tried to listen in on our conversations).

I checked behind me to make sure the door to my room was firmly shut.

"I can't wait for Saturday," I whispered. "I'm going to … Um, I'm going to ask my parents tonight if they can leave the house."

There was a silence, and I imagined Fred also checking to make sure no one could hear us … except he didn't say anything.

"So we can, um … sleep together," I said, feeling my heart banging in my chest.

Again there was silence, and then he cleared his throat.

"Are you not alone?" I asked.

"No, no. I'm alone."

A strange pit was forming in my stomach. Why wasn't he saying anything?

"What's going on, Fred?"

I heard him sigh.

"It's just that ... I'm not sure anymore."

His words were like an ice-cold shower.

"Not sure about what?" I finally managed to choke out.

An eternity passed.

"I'm not sure I want to make love," he finally blurted.

Everything started to spin in slow motion, and his words echoed in my head.

"You don't want to make love on Saturday? Or, like ... ever?"

He took a few seconds to answer.

"Just ... not right away."

I felt like there was a big empty hole in my heart and beneath my feet.

My boyfriend didn't want to have sex with me.

My father's words were playing like a loop in my head: *A guy is always ready.*

My father was the person I trusted more than anyone in the world, and I knew he'd told me the truth. So if it was really true that guys always wanted sex but my own boyfriend did not, the only logical explanation was that he didn't love me anymore, or at least didn't find me attractive enough.

Was it my breasts? I hardly had any compared to other

girls my age, and I'd always had a bit of a complex about it. Or was it my nose, which was a bit too long and bumpy and gave me a funny profile? Or had I said or done something that made him change his mind?

"Oh, okay ... I ... I have to go. Bye," I stammered in a tight voice.

"Bye," he muttered, without trying to keep me on the phone.

*

My hands were shaking, my pulse was beating hard in my ears, my stomach was churning in every direction at once.

Two toxic thoughts played ping-pong in my head. He doesn't love you. And you're not pretty enough.

I replayed our last moments over and over, especially the time down in Simon's storage room. I was sure I felt his erection against my leg while we were kissing.

But maybe I just imagined that? Or maybe it was just the bump of his wallet, which I mistook for a sign of arousal.

I wanted to talk to someone about it, but who? All my friends were virgins, so I felt like I had absolutely no one to turn to. And there was no way I'd go to my parents about this! I had no desire to listen to them confirm what I didn't want to hear: "Sweetie, you're going to have to consider that Frédéric may not like you as much as you like him ..."

I had no idea what to do. Did I still have a boyfriend, even? Maybe telling me that he didn't want to sleep with me was his way of breaking up with me?

Hurt and confused, I brooded all evening and all through the next day.

Friday night, I was browsing the internet looking for a distraction when I received a message from my friend Ellie asking me what was new.

Ellie and I have a bit of a special relationship. She was my babysitter when I was little, then she became a friend of the family, before turning into some sort of cosmic big sister. With nine years between us, I always had the impression that she knew everything there was to know about life, and that she could answer all my existential questions.

When I saw her name pop up on my screen, I wondered why I hadn't thought of her before and called her immediately.

"Hi! I'm so glad you called me," she answered happily.

"Hi, Ellie ..." I muttered, my heart heavy.

"Oh, no. What's going on?"

I couldn't hold back my tears.

"It's Fred ... I think it's over."

She gasped.

"Oh, no. Are you serious? What happened?"

I told her everything. About our plan to have sex tomorrow and his completely unexpected change of heart. I sobbed that I was convinced that Fred didn't think

I was pretty enough to sleep with and that backing out was his way of dumping me.

When I had finally unloaded everything on her, there was a little silence, and then Ellie ... laughed.

I wanted to hang up on her. Here I was, living through the worst moment of my entire life, and she thought it was funny!

"My darling friend," she said softly. "Your boyfriend doesn't want to leave you."

"How do you know?"

"I know because I was sixteen once, too. Plus you are heart-stoppingly beautiful, so stop imagining the opposite right now."

I was confused.

"So then why doesn't Fred want to have sex with me?"

"Because he's freaking out. It's that simple. Right now, he's also afraid that you don't find him attractive, or he's stressed about not being able to get an erection with you, or he's afraid that he doesn't know what to do and that he'll hurt you, or maybe all those things at the same time!"

I was in shock. Did that mean that ... guys could also not be ready to have sex?

"You think so?" I whispered.

"I don't think. I know it!" Ellie said in a reassuring voice.

*

The next day, I knocked on the door of my boyfriend's house, my hands damp and my heart pounding. We hadn't spoken since he told me he'd changed his mind, and I really hoped he wouldn't be upset by my long silence.

When he saw me at the door, Fred took me in his arms and kissed me for a long time, until butterflies were fluttering everywhere in my stomach and my heart.

"I'm sorry!" I said right away. "I didn't know how to react, because I thought that guys were always ready, and then I thought that the fact that you weren't meant that you didn't think I was attractive. But I understand I was wrong. We don't have to have sex now. I love you, so all I want is for us to be together."

He hugged me a bit tighter.

"I love you so much," he whispered in my ear.

He led me to his room and closed the door behind him. Our lips continued to dance together for a while. Our hands began to explore each other's bodies impatiently, becoming more and more intense. That sweet heat came into my belly again.

Slowly, nervously, we started to undress each other. First with our eyes and then removing every layer that stood between our skin.

We ended up completely naked together for the first time, and if I had any doubts about his desire for me a few days ago, his body provided very clear proof otherwise. And even though I'd been so confident, so impatient for this moment, I suddenly felt very vulnerable being exposed like this.

His fingers stroked my skin, and his soft eyes looked deeply into mine.

"You are so beautiful. I don't want to wait anymore."

I smiled.

"Are you sure?"

He nodded, before placing his mouth over mine at the very moment when ...

"FRED! WHERE DID YOU PUT MY PLAYSTATION CONTROLLER?" screamed my boyfriend's little sister just on the other side of the bedroom door.

We sat up so fast that our heads banged against each other.

"Ow!" we both cried out at the same time.

"FRED!" his sister insisted.

"I ... I don't know!" he stammered, leaping up to lock his door.

"BUT I NEED IT! I NEED THE CONTROLLER!"

"Melissa, I'm busy right now!"

"Busy doing disgusting things with your girlfriend!" shouted his little brother, who was passing by.

"Kids! Leave your brother alone!" their mother called from the kitchen.

"Come and help me with the groceries," added their father from the front hall.

Fred buried his face in his hands.

"Oh my God ... I'm sorry."

I couldn't help myself and burst out laughing. Fred also started to laugh, until we were both crying with laughter for several minutes.

"It might be easier to do this at your place," he said finally.

"Yeah, it might."

*

Convincing my parents to let me have the house wasn't too complicated. It was important to them that my first time took place in a secure environment where I would feel comfortable. So they went and organized a couple's day the next day without asking me any questions or giving me unsolicited advice, which I really appreciated. I felt lucky that this was so simple with them, because that wasn't the case with most of my friends and their parents.

Except that morning, while I was trying to read a book to help me relax before Fred arrived, my mother knocked on my door holding a huge beach towel.

"Hi, my darling. Do you want to help me with this?"

I frowned.

"Help you do what?"

She waved the towel.

"Spread this out."

She turned to my bed and began to strip off the sheets. I watched her for a few seconds, puzzled.

"Uh … what are you doing?"

"It's because blood stains terribly. It would be too bad if you soiled the mattress. Come on, help me!"

Even today, I think nothing can top the embarrassment of helping my mother install my kiddie beach towel under my mattress cover in preparation for the imminent rupture of my hymen. Nothing.

"Oh no, there are lumps," my mother said. "You won't be comfortable when you —"

I didn't let her finish.

"Okay!" I said a bit too loudly. "I can get rid of the lumps myself, thanks!"

My mother nodded and stared at me for a few seconds, smiling.

"My big girl is becoming a woman ... I can't believe it."

"Yup, that's right, really super. Okaythanksbyenow!"

My mother left, and I lay back on the bed, thinking that my parents could have been just a teeny bit less openminded, and I wouldn't have thought any less of them.

*

"You'll see, he might not be able to get hard at all."

"Or maybe he'll lose his erection along the way."

"He might also come in two seconds."

"Anyway, one thing's for sure: the first time is always over quickly."

We hear all sorts of things about the so-called first time before we actually experience it ourselves. The reality is that it's all true and all false at the same time. Whether it's amazing or a complete failure, every first time is unique, and there's no instruction manual to teach you how to prepare for the big moment.

So when Fred and I lay in each other's arms naked on the bed, I was flooded by a weird mix of emotions. I was restless, nervous, scared, excited and, especially, in love.

"Do you still want to?" my boyfriend whispered.

"Yes. Do you?"

He nodded and smiled, before slipping into me as gently as possible. I was surprised by the pain, but he was careful to go at my pace and everything went smoothly, with lots of love and tenderness. I was happy to be sharing this moment with him, even if it was far from perfect.

While I didn't expect to experience some great ecstasy, I admit that I was kind of hoping for it just a little. Frédéric was gentle and attentive, but my body felt overwhelmed by a flood of new sensations, making it hard for me to fully enjoy what was happening.

After about forty minutes of coming and going (more like going and not coming, frankly), I started to resent everyone who had ever told me that a first time is always quick. My crotch felt like it had been rubbed raw, and I just wanted one thing—for it to be over as fast as possible.

"Do you think you'll need much longer?" I finally asked.

My boyfriend's expression suddenly changed.

"I ... I was waiting for you to come with me ..." he stammered.

I smiled.

"You're sweet, Fred. But you don't have to wait. I'm not sure it's going to work for me."

He smiled back and slowly pulled out before lying down beside me.

"There are other ways."

Fred gave me a sly look and ran his hand down my belly to my crotch. He pressed his mouth against my ear and murmured "I love you," over and over.

My heart started to beat hard — very hard — then desire came rushing back like a fire in my lower belly, and my boyfriend ran his fingers down where no one had ever touched me before.

Then after several minutes, it came — that great ecstasy I had dreamed about.

And that's how my first time finished. As I lay back against Fred, I told myself that it was a far cry from what you see in the movies. Penetration didn't seem particularly pleasant to me, but I'd had a taste of a whole world of possibilities — to explore, to feel pleasure and give it to someone else.

As my eyes slowly closed, I told myself that I was looking forward to discovering everything that lay ahead of me.

And then I drifted off to sleep, already dreaming about my second time with him.

This Ain't Your Grandpa's Pipe
Nicolas Michon

Fuck.

Oh, man. Ok. This is it.

I'm two seconds away from giving my first blow job.

I'm on my knees in front of him.

Don't know how we got here. Half an hour ago we were out in the pool and then we came back in to dry off and get dressed and after that we ate Doritos on the couch and then …

Don't know how we started making out but now my face is twelve inches away from his dick and it's hard as a tree trunk and smells kind of like …

From now on, the smell of Doritos and chlorine is always gonna turn me on.

He's sitting here on my parents' ugly blue couch in our basement in Rosemère. Dad's out. If he came home and caught us he would flip out, like I'm some little kid acting up even though I'm sixteen. Even if I know for sure that what ~~I'm about to~~ we're about to do is totally ... good ... it's good and beautiful and ... and fucking hot and ...

My dad is super protective. Maybe because I'm adopted or something. I don't think my mother would have freaked out but she died of lung cancer last year and ...

Whatever. I'm two seconds away from giving my first blow job. From tasting my first penis. I'm finally going to find out if I like it. Maybe I won't ... at least ... well, maybe not the first time. Maybe I'll try again later. Maybe I won't. Maybe I'll ...

But I think I'm going to. Like it, I mean. I'm pretty sure. I've been dreaming about it for so long.

Christ, this is stressing me out. Ten years from now I bet I'll look back and say of course you were nervous you little asshole. It's normal. It was your first fellatio ... it's a big deal for fuck's sake.

Or maybe I won't remember this at all. I mean, I hope I do, but ...

                For fuck's sake, Jung-Woo, shut up already.
                          Chill, breathe ...

I pull off his pants. He pulls off his ironic Olivia Newton-John T-shirt. Lifts his hips to take off his briefs (my uncle Kevin is the only other guy I know who wears underwear like this). I pull off his socks one at a time and chuck them onto my father's desk.

 I turn back and look up. And there he is in all his glory ... looking like ... like a fucking god.

 The image in front of me is a billion times more exciting and more beautiful than all the porn and Michelangelo sculptures from art class. And God knows I've seen my share of sculptures and porn.

/   /   /   /

/   /   /   /

/   /   /   /

/   /   /   /

"You ok?"
"Totally. You?"
"Totally."
"K."

So. We're both ok. Good to know.

Ok. So. What am I doing here? I open my mouth. Snap it shut. Lick my lips. Look at him.

It's happening and it's happening fast, kind of like when I drank that Goldschläger at Mathilda's except now I don't feel like I'm going to puke, I feel like I'm going to … well … like …

A little laugh escapes from my throat. Mikael looks at me and smiles.

Good sign, right? That he's smiling?

Back to business.

Ok, whew, but I still don't know what to do.

Fuck, I just made a rhyme …

For starters, I'll grab it. Maybe lick the tip? The balls? It's all kinda complicated … no wait … how about …

I give him a little flick on the side of the shaft.

"Ow!"

"Oh sorry! It just happened!"

"Are you ok?"

"Yeah, sure … uh … I just don't know where to, like, start …"

"No problem. My grandpa would say, start with the basics."

Always a good place to start, with the basics. His grandpa is right.

Why is he talking to me about his grandpa?

Hey, whoa! Don't go there. Come on, man, stay focused. Eyes on the prize.

Ok, ok, the basics. I'll go on three.
One.
Two.
Three. Go!
"Agh! Not so hard!"
"Oh my God, sorry!"
"Haha, no, no it's me!"
"No it's me."
"Well ... yeah ..."
"Ok."
"What?"
"Sorry!"
"It's cool."
"Haha. It's just I'm kinda ... nervous. Sorry."
"Don't apologize. I'm the one who's ..."
"Well, that makes two of us."
"Right."
Ok, so I'll take it slower. With the basics. I squeeze it a bit, then a bit more but not too much. Ok, I can tell from his face and from his breathing that it's the right amount of pressure. But it's complicated. I'll just stay like this for a bit.

Wow. I can feel his blood pulsing in my palm.

He takes another deep breath. Is he breathing in or out? I can't tell. It's like surprise breathing.

I'm harder than I've ever been. There's a bit of juice leaking from his dick onto my hand. I want to taste it. Soon, soon. One thing at a time.

I start to jerk him off.

He smiles at me. It's funny seeing him look at me like this, his chin all tucked into his neck. Like a turtle, but I find it kinda hot anyway.

He's great, Mikael. He's the only friend I see outside of boarding school. We don't live close, but for the past two summers he's spent a week at our place and I've spent a week at his.

I'm glad he's my first blow job. My first dick. My first guy.

We're not lovers or anything. Just friends, but I'm happy it's him. He's not even gay. He has a girlfriend. He might be bi. Or pan. Or curious. I don't give two shits how he identifies. Well, I care, but it doesn't make any difference to me.

I had a girlfriend once but I wasn't in love with her. And I'm not in love with Mika. Unless ... maybe ... he's in love with me.

But we don't give a shit about all that. The important thing is that his name is Mikael, he's my bud, and we're doing something cool here in my parents' basement.

And ok, yeah, something I'll remember.

It's not the first time we've been totally naked together. I mean, apart from the locker room or the showers or the dorm. Once the Brothers took us camping near the

Gatineau and we took off from the others to go swimming in Lac Vert. That's what I was thinking about later when we had to write an essay for class. We had to use the second person. I still know it by heart.

Funny how when you remember something exactly you say "by heart," like it's in your heart instead of your head.

Here you are lying in the grass, fingers laced together, palms on your stomach like a corpse in a coffin. I feel you breathing against my side. Your head is resting against my chest and my left arm is wrapped around your fragile shoulder as if to protect you from everything complicated or mean. My hand strokes your forearm covered with dry twigs. The tips of my fingers feel the softness of your skin, so precious, dark from the August sun. I brush off a ladybug trying to camouflage itself among your freckles. The wind rustles your long hair against my cheek and the perfume of your scalp drifts into my nostrils before imprinting itself forever in my memory. You rub your feet against mine. The sand makes them rough but I cherish every scratch. You laugh. I laugh. We laugh. I place a kiss on your warm forehead. You're breathing is deep and I know you're smiling without even looking at you. You say, "That cloud looks like a fish cake." I say it looks more like a dry turd. We burst out laughing. You lift your head and you kiss me because you like that I'm funny. Your lips taste of sweat, your breath smells of cigarettes and your tongue ... your tongue.

In the distance my girlfriend is calling us: "Come on,

guys, hot dogs are almost ready! Hurry up and get dressed. We're going to join the others!"

Obviously, this is not the assignment I handed in to Brother Joseph. Instead I wrote some piece of junk about a guy who went mad because he mistook his own reflection in the mirror for his twin brother who died a year before. It was complete shit but I got an A.

Hey, I think about death a lot.

Focus, Jung-Woo, focus!

I focus. I've been jerking him off for a while and I want more. I move closer to his crotch. I lick my lips because a) they get chapped really easy and b) what I see gives me an appetite, like I'm looking at a nice yummy roast beef and now I'm starving. The smell of him makes its way up my nose and right into my brain. I close my eyes to sink into the smell and I ...

/ / / /

/ / / /

/ / / /

"You ok?"
"Oh my God, sorry. I was … somewhere else."
"Oh … ok. Where?"
"In the … smell."
"Of Doritos?"
"The other smell."
"Yeah, it does smell kind of mildewy down here."
"No, nonono. The smell of your …"
"Ah! Hahaha. The smell of my …"
"Yeah but … no, well … we get that moldy smell when the basement floods in the spring but my dad hasn't installed the dehumidificator yet so it's …"
"You mean dehumidifier?"
"Uh … yeah. That's what I meant but it's not an easy word to …"

Wink.

Nervous laughter.

/   /   /   /

FUUUUUUUUUCK! What the fuck are you talking about, you fucking asshole? "My dad hasn't installed the dehumidifiblafuckercator not an easy word to blahblahblah …"
Shut your fucking mouth!

"Haha, you're pretty cute."

/ / / /

Whew.
At least I'm cute.
Even though I don't actually think
I'm that good-looking
and I know I'm not that tall but Mika thinks
I'm cute anyway.
Cool!

Wait a sec. Are you in love?

Of course not. Obviously.

He bends down, takes my face between his hands and kisses me. Maybe he's just trying to make me feel like I don't have to worry, that he chose me to do this with him too.

But his hands are on my head and pushing my face toward his low belly.

"Hey, whoa. Don't push me."
"Sorry!"
"Yeah, well, I don't like it."
"Agh I'm sorry!"

"No big deal, but don't do it again."
"Ok."

/ / / /

Goddammit! Why did I say that? What's the matter with me? Maybe he was just trying to tell me to keep going? But then why didn't he just say so instead of forcing me? It's a turnoff. I mean, I still want to, but does he? God, I hate myself!

"Jung-Woo, I'm really sorry."
"It's ok."
"It's because … because I … you turn me on so much and I'm in a hurry and I don't know how to …"
"I'm in a hurry too but it's no reason to force me."
"Yeah I get it, I wouldn't like it either and now I'm afraid you won't want to do it anymore because I'm such an asshole."
"No, I still want to. Just give me a minute, asshole."
"Ok."
"K."

/ / / /

/ / / /

My cock goes soft. So does his.
It's probably that mildew smell ...

/ / / /

/ / / /

"I'm nervous and I got carried away."
"It's ok. Me too. I just don't want to rush. It's my first time."
"Mine too."

                                            Say what??

/ / / /

"What?"
"Yeah ... I don't do this with my girlfriend."
"How come?"

/   /   /   /

"Because ... because of I'm not in love with her."

/   /   /   /

/   /   /   /

"You don't say 'because of.'"
"What?"
"You say that all the time. It's just 'because,' not 'because of.' Would you say 'when of'?"
"No."
"So don't keep saying 'because of.'"
"Ok."
"Fuck ... you don't love her?"
"No."

/   /   /   /

/   /   /   /

/ / / /

/ / / /

"It's because no one's talking and I'm completely naked and you have all your clothes on."

/ / / /

"Hahahaha!"
"Hahaha!"
"By the way, you have really soft hair."

/ / / /

"Is this turning you on too much?"

He looks at me. I smile at him. He climbs on top of me like he's riding a horse. I grab his ass with both hands. His butt is hard but soft … a bit hairy … hairier than mine at any rate. He puts his lips gently on mine. Our lips match our movements while his hands undress me. It's slow and easy but in two seconds I'm going to be stark naked and he'll be able to see every hair on my body which is like, seven of them.

His stomach is soft on mine. His dick swells again and I feel it grow against my belly.

I hate my belly.

"I love your belly."

I no longer hate my stomach.

Mika starts to kiss my cheeks, my ears. I feel his tongue go in and I hear myself groan. He starts to bite my earlobes ... my hands dig into his back ... I scratch his shoulder blades, he bites my neck but ...

"Too much!"

"Christ, you really aren't good with force!"

"Sorry."

"Keep going."

We wrap our arms around each other and his mouth finds mine and we sink into it, squeeze each other hard, almost until I can't breathe. We're all lips and tongue and our parts rub against each other and I feel his heart beat so hard against my chest that I confuse it with my own and ...

I have never felt good like this.

Is he feeling good?

"Are you ok?"

"Never felt so good."

The answer was fast like quick-fire, like we need to ask and answer about everything before our mouths can keep making love.

Shit. Are we making love? Am I in love? I don't think

so. But maybe I am. Can you be in love, like, just for right now? Just for this moment? Just because you feel that another person wants you as much as you want him? Can you be lovers who are ... like ... equals but who, like, share a mutual desire ... who can give and receive ... consume and be consumed and ...

        Shit, so now you're a fucking poet?

    What time is it? Was that a noise upstairs? Is it my father? Mikael, are you in love with me? Of course you're not. But are you sure? Are you asking yourself the same thing? Are you gay? Who gives a shit? Do we give a shit? Anyway ... he would obviously not be doing what we're doing right now if he was a thousand percent straight. Does he know that? That he's not straight?

Agh, my head is spinning ...

And it stops spinning when he grabs both of our cocks together in his hand.

"Ahhhhh!"

He starts to jerk us off together while he kisses my mouth and neck. I'm sweating. He licks my side right up to my armpit. My sweat's running like ice cream down the side of a cone and he kisses me so I can taste it too. It disgusts me a bit. I've never tasted my own sweat because I'm not a psychopath but mixed with his saliva and seeing the effect this has on him the idea bothers me less and less and then ...

His mouth goes back to my neck, my chest, my nipple ...

HHHHHOOOLLLY fuck!

"AAAAAaaaaah mmmmmmm! Fuck, where did you learn how to do that?"

"My girlfriend. Uh, it's a big erogenous zone for girls and for some guys too."

"Have you already done this with other guys?"

"Nope. Finding out about it right here."

> Finding out that my nipples are an erogenous zone.

"Cool. Keep going?"

"Fuck yeah."

His pleasure in giving me pleasure grows along with my pleasure at having him nibble on my nipples. While his mouth is busy with one, his fingers play with the other.

I sweat, he licks. The more I sweat, the more he licks, the more he sweats. The smell of his perspiration makes me harder — like I can't get any harder, and …

Mikael moves down along my stomach that I don't hate anymore. He puts his tongue in my navel and it has the same effect as it did on my ears and …

He keeps going … down.

He takes my cock in his hand.

Looks up at me.

Smiles.

Licks the tip.

Opens his mouth and …

/ / / /

/ / / /

I sink deeper and deeper into the sofa.

/ / / /

/ / / /

/ / / /

And it's weird but …
I mean, I really like it, but it's not …

It's not …
It's not like I thought.
I mean it's fun but it's not …
I don't know …
It's fucking hot,
but I expected …
not more exactly but …

                              Uh, ok, that's it …

            /   /   /   /

            /   /   /   /

    Mikael lifts my legs and pushes my knees toward my face. I'm watching him.
    "What are you doing?"
    "Uh, nothing."
    "What?"
    "I dunno …"
    "Are you going to …"
    "Well I … I wanted … I wanted to taste …"
    "Agh, am I talking too much? Like, asking too many questions?"
    "No, but you're making me nervous."
    "Oh. Sorry."
    He lets my legs drop.

                    Great. Couldn't keep your big mouth shut, eh, you big asshole?

    "Do you trust me?"
    "What?"

"Do you trust me?"
"Haha. Yes, Aladdin."
"Aladdin?"
"Um. You haven't seen the movie?"
"No."
"In the film he asks Jasmine if she trusts him before he takes her on the magic carpet and ..."

                              Big. Fucking. Deal.

"Can't I just eat your ass without talking about Walt Disney?"
"Well, you were talking about your grandfather."
"What?"
"You said that ..."
"Yeah I know. I was sorry after."
"Hahaha, it doesn't matter!"
"Hahaha."
"In fact, could you ... keep going?"
"... Yes."
"Because ... because I've been thinking about this for a while ... well, not thinking about it but ... I feel like, well ... trying it ... with you."

A pause. He smiles.

I kiss him. He kisses me back. Goes back to tracing a path on my neck, my chest, my belly which I like now, my dick. His mouth goes down to my balls. Big moan. He keeps going lower and his tongue finds my hole and ...

                               FU
                            CKING
                           HELL!!!
                           My anus
            is also a fucking erogenous zone!

   His tongue in my ear and my bellybutton was already
bliss, but this? This is fucking paradise.

    /   /   /   /

    /   /   /   /

    /   /   /   /

    /   /   /   /

    /   /   /   /

   My eyes sink deep behind my eyelids. I moan so loud that at one point he stops.
   "Does it hurt?"

"Don't stop!"
He keeps going. I feel dizzy. Every time I look down I see him looking right at me and the smile in his eyes makes me completely crazy especially because I can feel him getting off at the same time. We are jerking off to the same rhythm.
"You can pull my hair."
I pull his hair.
"Too hard?"
"No."
"Harder?"
"No."
"Can I put my hands behind your head and push?"
"If you want."
"I want."
"Go."

/ / / /

"Let me go deeper."
"I'm afraid I'll fart."
"HAHAHAHAHAHAHAAA!"
"Hahahahaha!"
"You won't fart."
"Aren't you afraid I'll relax too much?"
"Control yourself and it won't happen."

He keeps going. I take a deep breath and try to think about nothing, just concentrate on my breathing and what I'm feeling, try to relax and control myself at the same time.

It's not easy. Let yourself go and everything will be fine. Breathe. Relax. Everything will be fine. Sweet ...

I let him go in a bit deeper with his tongue. I'm still scared but I don't think I'm going to fart in his mouth. He moans, which makes me moan.

I think I like this. I think I like this. Yeah ok I like this. I give into it more and more. My head is spinning but I'm letting go at the same time. At least I think I am. It's weird but I have never been this turned on. It's too good. I can't believe this is happening to me. With him. I'm losing my mind and thinking of nothing both at the same time. My head is going to explode along with my penis and ...

"Mik, I'm going to cum."

But all I can hear is more moaning that is getting me more and more excited ...

"Mik, if you don't stop I'm going to shoot off."

/ / / /

Mikael doesn't stop.

It's everywhere. It's all over my stomach that I now like. Mikael stands up.

It's everywhere on his stomach too except it's his and …

"It's all over the floor. Do you have a towel?"

"Later."

He climbs on top of me, lays his whole body on top of mine. Our wet dicks meet and kiss just like our mouths.

"What time is your dad coming home?"

"Dunno."

"K."

"We still have time."

"Yay."

A few slashes.

"Jung-Woo?"

More slashes.

"Yeah?"

More slashes.

"Are you in love with me?"

A million slashes but super close together and fucking nervous ...

"No."

"Ah ..."

Ah?
What's with Ah?
What does AH mean?

"You?"

"Nah."

"K."

"K."

Slashes to fill the silence that hides the truth.

His body moves away from mine. He grabs the bag of chips and eats a few. He sits beside me but not too close. A bit too far away.

Then he lifts his legs and rests them on top of mine.

"Do you think Elio felt the same way in *Call Me by Your Name*?"

"What?" His mouth is full.

"It's a movie."

"Haven't seen it." (Mouth full.)

"Actually it's a book but they made it into a movie."

"K." (Mouth full.) "You like movies, huh?" (Mouth empty.)

"Yeah. Anyway ..."

He smiles at me. My turn to climb on top of him. I kiss him. My turn to explore his body with my mouth, which now tastes like chips. Mmmmmmm. His skin. His nipples. I don't like his sweat as much as he likes mine, but to each his own taste.

Shut the fuck up, Grandma.

I go lower and lower, and lower still ...

/   /   /   /

/   /   /   /

/   /   /   /

/   /   /   /

Just when I'm kneeling between his legs, my knees slip on his cum and I end up ass over teakettle on the floor.

"Fuck man, are you ok?"

"Hahahahaha, yes!"

"Hey, boy, you nearly went ass over teakettle right there!"

He said ass over teakettle!

We laugh. I pick up my T-shirt that he threw beside the sofa and use it to wipe up the mess. Except it's not dirty. It's natural. All of this is perfectly natural. I get up to go hide my shirt under my bed.

"Where are you going?"

"I'll be back."

"Putting your T-shirt in the laundry?"

"Yeah, sure."

Fucking liar.

I come back. He smiles. I go over and kneel down where I was, ready to do whatever I was about to do.

"Wait a sec. Kiss me, Jung-Woo."

I kiss him. We kiss. I move my hands all over his body,

and my mouth follows my hands. Neck. Chest. Nipples. Belly. Navel. Below the navel.
 Fuck.
 Oh man. Ok. This is it.
 I'm two seconds away from giving my first blow job.

Leap into the Unknown
Vanessa Duchel

March 15, 1989, 1:01 p.m.

In the hospital, people around me are screaming. There is weeping, too. Tears of joy. Finally, I dare to believe it's time. I sense a bright light. I was in the dark just a few minutes ago and suddenly there are new colors, smells and warmth around me.

I am being delivered, so to speak, from a very comfortable place where I have been cradled for a long time.

It goes without saying that the first time you're born will also be the last. This traumatic event will never happen again. Fortunately.

First times that involve leaps into the unknown are scary.

And I am a fearful person. I'm afraid of everything, filled with anxiety in general. Having to face something new is deeply stressful for me.

Spring 2015

This is when I decided that I wanted to meet girls on the dating app. At the ripe old age of twenty-six, I gave in to my curiosity for the first time. I was not opposed to the idea of kissing a woman. I allowed myself to imagine a love that was entirely female.

I started swiping a lot. I wanted to find the girl who would know how to make me change teams. I was searching for her, and it was eating me up inside.

The idea turned me on. All those questions I'd been asking myself for years would finally be answered. *Does a girl kiss like a guy? Will I be attracted to her? Will I compare my body to hers? Will we understand each other better than a guy and a girl? Do lesbian couples assume gender roles? Will I be able to fall in love? Do I have the guts to go through with this? And what about my friends? How will they react?*

It made me dizzy. I was feeling romantic. Like the star of a film that nobody knew the ending to. My life was going to take a new turn, and I was really hoping to meet my costar.

The first girl who was a match — let's call her Rose — was very tiny. She weighed about half as much as me. And right there I answered one of my own questions. Yes, I will compare myself to her. I analyzed her body and didn't even dare think about the two of us wrapped together. I would crush her! How could we have a relationship if we were so different physically?

Plus, she was pretty, which intimidated me. Pretty and, soon, the first girl to push me against the wall of a karaoke bar bathroom to kiss me. A great kisser, dammit. And gorgeous, too.

I was feeling good. Stressed out, but good. I was feeling hornier than ever. But those questions were still lurking in a corner of my brain. Have I always been a lesbian? Was I now bisexual?

More questions than can be answered with a single kiss. Because later that same evening, Rose left me alone on a street corner in the gay village. It was the first time I wanted to hold on to my desire to be with a woman.

We sexted and exchanged intimate photos a few weeks later. I'd never received anything like this from a girl. I felt like some kind of sex offender. As if I didn't have the right to look at her breasts, her vulva. I admired them anyway. I wanted to touch them, stroke them. I wanted to feel her naked against me. I was both in a hurry and afraid to make love with a woman for the first time.

But it wouldn't happen with Rose.

Not long after that, I matched with Jasmina on the same site. We met up right away. She was really nice. She was a lesbian, but her parents didn't know. She was afraid of telling them. I tried to tell her that I understood her fear of confessing her sexual orientation, when the truth is that I didn't understand at all. I had no idea about the prejudices of her family or her parents' beliefs. It must be hard to love someone and at the same time be afraid of losing the love of your own family. Who would you choose in a case like that?

Poor Jasmina, pulled between two separate worlds. It broke my heart. I always dropped her off a block from her house to make sure no one would see us kissing before she went back to her parents, pretending she'd just been on a date with Cédrick.

The two of us had good chemistry. It was the first time I'd had an intimate relationship with a woman. And when I say intimate, I mean more than kissing. It wasn't love yet, but things were moving along. I was allowing myself to open a door. The door to the possibility of a same-sex romance. I surprised myself thinking about the pros and cons of our relationship. Maybe we'd be good together? Our lips met softly, and we didn't obsess over comparing our bodies. It was good. It was special. It felt like me, right now.

I was still tantalized by the fact that I hadn't yet made love. *We* still hadn't made love. But I had a block about it, and it was really stressing me out. I'd never done that — slept with a girl — and deep down I was afraid I'd be no good at it. Scared I wouldn't be able to get into it, afraid I wouldn't know how to make her come.

She kept saying, "There's a first time for everything.

It isn't a problem, we can take our time, you can take your time."

She was too nice. I felt a bit like I was taking advantage of her niceness. Like I was dangling the promise of a sexual future that I wasn't even sure about.

One evening when we got back to my place, after drinking a bit (too much) at the bar, we found ourselves making out passionately — making out like there was no tomorrow. As if our tongues were never going to be free from each other. I told myself I wanted to be vulnerable with her. I wanted her to feel me against her and inside her.

Everything was in place to make things happen the way we wanted.

I started with her mouth, then her neck. I felt the desire rising inside me, but I was afraid, too. I started to analyze every gesture, as if I was watching myself from above. My lips traced a path down her body and I didn't think they would stop — until there was a giant knot in my stomach. And this knot was talking to me. It was telling me I wasn't ready.

My head protested. It wanted to keep going. I had to break the ice, or at least melt it a bit. It was all or nothing. And it was now.

I felt Jasmina getting turned on. She was aroused by my touch. Her skin was soft and willing. I took the southern route that I was drawing in my head.

I was there. I put my hand on her panties. I caressed

her. As if I knew what I was doing. I stroked her breasts with my other hand.

To be honest, up to that point I thought I was doing well. All the signals told me that I was giving Jasmina pleasure. I was reassured.

But a few seconds later, I pulled my hand away from her crotch. I was afraid of reaching beneath the fabric. I was scared. What if I made a mistake about going inside? If I took too long to find the entry? It would be embarrassing. Did I absolutely have to go through with this? Would I look completely ridiculous once and for all?

I lost all my courage. I wasn't ready. I was too afraid of being ashamed. The worst thing was that I was embarrassed to be embarrassed. It was like being afraid of being afraid. It made no sense.

I had two or three more chances with Jasmina, but I was never able to go all the way. For almost a year now, I had been unable to do the thing I'd wanted and dreaded more than anything.

At the same time, I wasn't sleeping with men anymore. I only wanted relationships with women. I no longer wanted to please men. I admit I was still attracted to them, but women and my new "mission" were more important to me than spending one night with a guy.

And so after about seven or eight dates, Jasmina disappeared. Not a word or photo. I think I hurt her. I'd understood what we both wanted, but it was too much pressure. She never put this pressure on me. I was the one who had pushed her into my new same-sex relationship.

This first time made me grow up, just like the one before. These two stories formed me, put a big permanent stamp on my heart and on my head.

Summer 2016

After I quit the dating apps, I got up the nerve to contact a complete stranger on social media. I found her very attractive. Not just physically. She felt like freedom. She wanted to live life to the fullest and she looked the part. Always with a smile on her face, always living in the moment. It was admirable. Attractive.

Her name was Léa. I already liked her a lot just from what I saw on my phone. She made me feel relaxed and confident — something I'd been longing for since forever.

Next to her, I was stuck. I was afraid of everything. I'd stopped living and realized that I was even embarrassed to hope. But I did something I would have never allowed myself to do before. I wrote to her.

Hi Léa, I think we have friends in common. I don't know why I'm doing this but I would like to have a drink with you. Is that possible?

She said yes. I was already sweating. I felt like there was a mini sinkhole under my feet. What if she didn't find me interesting enough?

There was only one way to find out.

The evening went well. The looks we exchanged were as electrifying as P. K. Subban's passes, but not for the same reasons. We both felt the sexual tension.

"You're really my kind of girl," she told me, after we'd been talking for an hour.

Which meant what? That I was her type, okay, but how? Physically? Psychologically? How?

I didn't even have time to ask myself any more questions before she asked me straight out, "Are we going back to your place or mine?"

I invited Léa to my place. Léa who was kind and attractive. Léa who lived free.

We kissed each other on the stairs. She tasted soft, like clouds. Light and a bit sweet. I wanted her, wanted to get to know her. I tried to ignore the pressure that was already slowly but surely pressing down on my shoulders. I was losing my bearings in front of her. Everything was in place for the first time. She was very thin, but I didn't compare myself to her. She looked at me like I was something wonderful.

I knew she wanted me, too. I was already afraid of getting hurt. She was like a honeybee, this Léa. Buzzing around the flowers. Maybe I already loved her.

After this amazing night there were many more kisses.

Nights spent cuddled tightly together. I didn't want her to guess how much I wanted her, even though deep down she already knew. I let her come to me. I didn't want her to realize that my life had revolved around her for the past two weeks. I missed calls, I drove her everywhere even when she didn't ask me to, I listened to her, she listened to me, we drank, we invited each other over, we were enough for one another.

The opportunity to make love presented itself more than once. She even told me she wanted to. She wanted it, too. My head kept telling me that these invitations to make love together couldn't be possible. I think I thought she was too good for me. Too beautiful for me. Why would she like me? I was afraid to give in to it.

It was only two years later that I dared to admit to her that I had been crazy about her. That I saw her everywhere, that I wanted to devour her whole.

She had met someone. A nice guy. This news shocked me. I should have taken a chance.

It was the first time I had reached out to someone outside of dating sites, and I tortured myself with the rejection. Léa meant so much to me. Today I'm still trying to find a way to be free, but she encouraged me to see my true value, and to love myself more.

Except that I still hadn't slept with a girl.

Would I ever get over my anxiety about touching a woman and my fear of making a mistake? I no longer believed it.

After Léa, there were several years of being celibate, of questioning, introspection, unsuccessful encounters with men and a few dry kisses in bars with girls I never saw again.

June 2020

One spring followed another until I was thirty-one years old. On a whim, I rejoined a dating site that I hadn't been on in months. It had been a long dry spell for romance. I'd almost given up on the idea of ever being with a woman.

And that's when I met her. The woman of my life.

Her.

For the first time, I could say it. Even after five minutes. She was everything I could wish for. She looked at me with loving eyes. Loved us — my body and me. It's difficult to explain the connection I had with her. Today I still don't know how to describe the emotions that she awoke in me. Even before we got to know each other, we were never apart. She was there, real and beautiful. We were passionate about one another, we passed our days exchanging looks that were both innocent and filled with desire. We felt equally the need to touch each other, to discover and learn about each other. My lips never got tired of hers.

It was simple. I wanted to make her happy. I wanted everything we were feeling to come true. She taught me how to love.

Our first time was my first time. I finally let myself go there. I was still afraid, but the love was stronger than the anguish and stress. It was passionate, planned, mutual, intoxicating without alcohol. She accepted me in all my vulnerability, with kindness and respect. I was hardly afraid anymore of being judged. I was ready for her to teach me and guide me, without pride. Me, the proud one.

And what happened our first time? I was very average, below par. But it was my first time. Remember, we are only born once.

But this small trauma is now behind me. The ice is broken, I can leave the embarrassment behind.

For me, my body got in the way for a long time. My body and my head don't seem to understand that they can be desirable. That other bodies may want mine, want to enjoy it, caress it.

Ever since I was young, I've had a false relationship with intimacy. Too often I would act without validating the needs and desires of the other person because I refused to believe that they were being genuine. It's clear that I have a serious lack of self-confidence, and my body plainly shows it in how I react to others. I often ended a relationship because I was too insecure about the way I looked. This has put me in several uncomfortable situations, some healthy and some not. Not everyone reacts with empathy in such moments, but some do. And those are the moments you have to keep in your mind, in your heart.

Now I can only get better, with the help and love of my girlfriend. Because yes, she's my first girlfriend. My first love relationship.

Each of these four relationships, in their own way, has made my fears melt away. They broke through my discomfort and allowed me to learn more about myself and my sexual orientation. I would say little Vanessa did everything she could to avoid these moments over too many long years — even though she dreamed about them.

I often tell myself that I haven't wasted time, in spite of everything. That it had to happen like this. Sometimes anxiety took over my emotions and the way I experienced them during important moments of my life, but that's okay, because you have to take these things at your own pace.

Rose represents the first time I realized I was interested in women. Thanks to that relationship, I was able to confirm a lot of things. That it was possible for me to let myself be kissed and desired in public.

Jasmina represents the first time I allowed myself to think beyond just sexual attraction. The idea that a lasting love story with a woman was something I wanted and could be comfortable thinking about. Fear was part of this scenario for sure, but the important thing was to accept it. For too many years, this fear led me to doubt my own desires, made me sweep them under the carpet. The fear is still there, but it bothers me less.

Léa was the first time same-sex desire and romance

became perfectly clear for me. She wasn't the right person for me, but she let me imagine a romantic future that I didn't think was possible before, because I never allowed myself to see it through.

Now, looking back and with introspection, I want to say I'm pansexual. I go where my heart goes. It depends on who I'm interested in.

First times really aren't always easy. They're stressful, strange, anxiety-provoking, instructive, funny and/or sad.

But they allow each of us to move forward to happiness, one step at a time.

GOLIATH

The Great Fat Bird Migration
Olivier Simard

The living-room armchair was enormous. A gray and purple La-Z-Boy that my stepfather had bought at Corbeil. When I sat in it, I felt like I was lying in a giant baked potato.

It was a Friday, and my parents had gone to bed early. It was almost midnight. There were fewer and fewer good shows to watch on TV, but I was too lazy to get up and drag my body to my room, so I kept flipping channels.

Suddenly, between the weather and a commercial for microfiber dishcloths, images caught my attention.

The movies that were on after eleven were hardly ever worth watching, especially for a boy my age. I was fourteen. Normally I would have switched to a sports channel. I loved watching sports on TV, and when I had nothing else to do, I could watch the highlights two or three times in a row.

But that night, my enthusiasm for hockey, golf, synchronized swimming and Olympic ping-pong mysteriously vanished, because my whole attention was sucked in to the scene unfolding on the family television.

I pushed my glasses up on my nose and watched a woman bathing in the ocean. The salt water dripped from her damp hair. It streamed down her bare breasts.

I placed the remote on the armrest. Very slowly, without me even noticing, my hand slipped down into my pants. It nestled there comfortably, like a little fox happy to be in its warm den.

The commercial break made me jump. The TV volume was way too loud, and I quickly pressed the Mute button (with my other hand, because the first one flatly refused to come out of hiding). I heard the deep, regular snoring of my stepfather coming from the end of the hall.

It wasn't the first time I'd had an erection. I'd had them regularly since I was little and until now the experience was like a minor curiosity. Sometimes I'd stand in front of the mirror in the bathroom and amuse myself by pushing my penis down and then watching it spring up again. Or I would lie on my stomach and try to bend it down and squish it against my mattress. All for naught. My erect penis was as squishy and malleable as string cheese, unbreakable as a carbon-fiber hockey stick.

But that night, as I lay comfortably in the living-room armchair, something changed. This erection was different from the others. I was in a *very* big hurry for the commercials to come to an end.

When the movie finally started up again, things unfolded rapidly. A bearded captain landed his motorboat on the beach. Then he and the woman with the wet breasts got down to business. I squirmed around to pull my pants down my thighs. The springs of the armchair started to emit a high-pitched squeak. I listened for sounds coming from my parents' bedroom at the end of the hall — and heard a creaking sound, then another.

False alarm. It was just the old central heating starting up in the kitchen. I put the volume on low while on high alert for other noises in the house.

In my underwear, my right hand got to work. Weird how it knew exactly what to do. That lasted for about thirty seconds. Then there was an explosion. I closed my eyes. I had never felt my face scrunch up like that before.

It felt like a big flock of fat birds were flying out of my penis. Fat birds that soared over my belly and crashed straight into the lenses of my glasses.

I changed stations, turned off the TV and ran to the safety of my room. After finishing off a box of Kleenex to clean everything up, I took stock of my situation.

What had just happened exceeded anything I had experienced in my entire life. It was better than gym class. Better than Goliath, my favorite ride at La Ronde.

Better than a Deep'n Delicious cake or a Crispy Crunch Blizzard.

Better than a Saturday night playing *Call of Duty* at my cousin Gregory's house. A thousand times better, even.

That night, I did it twice more. Sitting in my parents' purple armchair, on the verge of exhaustion, my pants down by my knees, I had a revelation.

I had discovered my goal in life. From now on, I would try to reproduce this sensation as often as possible.

I would of course have preferred to carry out this project with someone else. A girl like the ones in my gym class who wore ponytails and rolled up their T-shirt sleeves. I thought they were magnificent, and I was in love with about half of them.

The problem was that as soon as I liked a girl, I would automatically stop talking to her and avoid all contact. I secretly hoped that would force her to take up the chase and make the first move. Which, obviously, never happened.

Given all this, being able to sleep with a real person was as impossible as taking a bath on the moon or reaching the middle of my back with my tongue. So while I waited for the blessed day when I would *finally* make love for the first time, I had no other choice.

I would have to fall back on the prodigious power of my own imagination.

Aunt Sylvie's Golf Balls

Inspired by my new passion, I started to observe the girls around me, to research erotic elements that might spice up my solitary romps. A slightly see-through blouse, the barely suggested shape of a breast under an oversized sweater, the delicate trace of a panty line through the seat of a pair of pants.

I stored away each of these little details. Then, when evening came, I would "remix" them to create perfect scenes. Scenarios that with a little elbow grease would send entire flocks of fat birds into my bedroom sky.

The cashier at the corner store liked to wear polo shirts, and she would only do up the first button. She was the owner's daughter, and a little older than me. During long quiet evening shifts, she would sit behind the counter and do her homework.

I imagined myself arriving with a bag of empties to return. The cashier would quietly close the door and flip over the BACK IN 5 MINUTES sign. Together we would go to the storeroom at the back, where we would make love in silence, standing in the middle of the beer bottles and milk crates.

I spied on the girls at school but also, and above all, on the adult women around me. For some reason that still escapes me, they were my favorites. Diane, my friend Steven's mother, wore flowy flowered dresses that came to the middle of her calves. Steven had a pool and I often saw her wearing a bathing suit. Diane's breasts were big and heavy. I imagined them to be fresh, moist and pure white, like cream cheese.

Madame Aziba was my French teacher. Her lips, like plump jujubes, hid large straight teeth. Madame Aziba wore stockings with flower patterns, feather earrings and long strings of pearls. Since there were two Victors in my class, she usually called me by my full name — Victor Labonté — and this kind of made me feel like I was her favorite. My dream was to make love to her after school in the little cupboard beside the board, where she kept the answers to the workbook questions, a bottle of spray cleaner and thirty-two copies of *Perfume*, by Patrick Süskind.

One day when I was looking through family souvenirs that my mother kept in a shoebox, I came across a veritable gold nugget — a photo of my Aunt Sylvie taking a bath. In the picture, taken about ten years earlier, Aunt Sylvie smiled at the camera with a glass of champagne in her hand. Her black bangs fell just above her eyes, and her open mouth showed off her astonishingly sharp canine teeth. Her breasts were shaped like bananas, with brown nipples pointing out to the front.

As I examined them closely, I calculated that each one would weigh just a bit more than a golf ball. Knowing that, I could imagine the exact feel of what it would be like to hold them in my hands.

In the photo, Aunt Sylvie was sitting down and you couldn't see her lower body, but I liked to imagine her standing. The warm water running down her thin, delicate legs. Her pubic hair covered in foam, and the slightly wrinkled skin of her bottom. The buttocks of a woman. I imagined kissing her and feeling her sharp teeth with the tip of my tongue. The slightly tangy taste of her saliva mixed with the champagne.

I grabbed the photo and hid it at the back of my sock drawer. From that day on, Aunt Sylvie became my number one muse. The undisputed star of my imaginary scenarios.

She had a catlike nature and rebellious personality that I found irresistible. There was something in her look, as if she was always hiding a secret thought that amused her but that she kept for herself. I also loved the way she talked. She used certain words that proved to me without a doubt that she was naughty — in the naughtiest sense of the word.

One Sunday in February I heard her talking on the phone when she came to lunch at the house, and the steamy kitchen was filled with the smell of toast and the gurgling of the coffee machine.

As usual, Aunt Sylvie was laughing a lot, but at one point she was surprised by something and said, "Well, fuck my ass," to the person on the line. I had never heard this expression, but I felt every syllable vibrate in my pants. Like the paws of a cat playing the piano between my legs.

Fuck. My. Ass.

My parents would never dare talk like that.

That night I imagined making love to Aunt Sylvie in every room in the house, in the garden shed and in the olive-green Westfalia that she and my uncle Patrick had bought to drive down to Fort Lauderdale.

The Masturbodrome

All week and weekend, at home and at school, I was constantly on the lookout for a quiet place to free the sparrows that were swarming around in my underwear. Since I was quite a good student, my teachers never minded when I politely asked for permission to go to the bathroom in the middle of class. I would go down the long empty hallways to the least busy bathrooms beside the music room. I would choose the stall farthest from the door and quickly get to work so I could return to class before raising suspicion. When someone walked in, I would have to stop and wait, my pants around my knees, until the intruder left and I had to start all over again.

But my hideout of choice at home was the shower. This steamy stall, hot and self-cleaning, was the supreme masturbodrome. Not only that, but the hot water fell loudly on the acrylic floor, producing a background roar that protected me from prying ears. I could take my time in the shower. Twenty long minutes before the water started to cool — a sign that the hot-water tank would soon be empty and it was time to wrap up the session.

Because I "washed" morning and night, I was quickly confronted by a new problem. My penis, raw from so much friction, would sometimes start to burn like a Merguez sausage.

If I wanted to keep up the pace, I needed top-quality lubricant. I started to try out different products that lined the bathroom shelves, beginning with my mother's dandruff shampoo. Its rich creamy texture did the job perfectly, but the little blue bottle with the orange cap quickly emptied after a few watery sessions.

I had to find something else.

After several moderately successful attempts, I finally discovered the product that would change my life. My stepfather, who was training for a marathon, would rub it on his inner thighs before a race to prevent chafing.

It was a stroke of genius. This yellowish jelly with a petroleum base gave me the perfect sensation and I could use as much as I wanted without ever feeling the slightest burn.

Before long, I decided that this huge jar of Vaseline was mine. I hid it in my sock drawer next to the photo of Aunt Sylvie.

Shame

Masturbation was now part of my daily routine, like eating two pieces of toast every morning or taking the bus to school. I indulged in it freely, without the slightest hesitation. It had become my refuge and my greatest passion.

However, a new feeling was preventing me from completely enjoying my favorite sport. I was consumed with shame.

I felt like there were two completely separate Victors inside me. On one side was the polite and well-raised boy who got good marks at school. Of course everyone loved that Victor.

And then there was the "other" Victor. A Victor sitting on the toilet, his mouth open and his pants lowered, touching himself while imagining adult women having an orgasm.

This Victor had to remain absolutely hidden. No one must discover his existence.

Constantly filled with the fear of being found out, I became a specialist in the art of camouflaging my activities. Like a serial killer who systematically gets rid of any trace of his murders, I had ways of doing things, my routine. I always acted in total silence and, at the end, I cleaned up the crime scene so well that it was often cleaner than when I arrived.

Looking back now, I have to admit that I was not as subtle as I thought at the time. The drastically reduced stock of dandruff shampoo and the mysterious disappearance of my stepfather's jar of Vaseline must have aroused suspicion. To say nothing of my endless showers and the wastebasket full of crusty tissues in my room.

But, hey, I was fourteen years old and I was convinced that *no one* in the entire world knew that I was a serial masturbator.

Mathias

At school, most of my friends were also fairly discreet about the subject. The only one who wasn't embarrassed about going on about it was Mathias. Even if most of his stories were no different from the ones that I myself experienced in the privacy of my room, listening to them come out of the mouth of someone else was both hilarious and disgusting. Not a lunch hour passed without one or two juicy anecdotes from Mathias. Like a little boy who was proud to show his parents that he was able to tie his shoelaces by himself or color inside the lines, Mathias had a constant need to remind us that he was practically a man.

One night when I went to sleep over at his place, he wanted to push the demonstration a bit further.

We were both sleeping on the sofa bed in the basement. After turning out the light, we had talked for a long time about the girls we liked. Mathias was hung up on Geneviève Lamontagne, the captain of the Budding Geniuses quiz team and also the person responsible for writing the horoscopes for the student paper.

As for me, I had a big crush on Martine Gagné, my deskmate in geography. Sometimes while the teacher was writing notes on the board, we would play Hangman in our notebooks. I had never professed my love for her and I had no intention of doing so. I was happy to keep my love for Martine a secret, well hidden by my sadness. Conveniently desperate.

Lying there in the dark, there was a moment when Mathias and I stopped talking. My eyes were closed but I was still thinking about Martine.

Suddenly I heard Mathias's voice.

"Hey, Vic ..."

"Hmmm?"

"You asleep?"

"What do you think?"

"I can't," he said after a moment. "When I think about Geneviève, all I want to do is whack off."

Even though we were each in our own sleeping bags, I could feel the pressure of his shoulder against mine.

"You feel like doing that ... now?" I asked.

"I have no choice, man. I can't help myself. You don't feel like it? Are you sure?"

The idea of masturbating beside my friend didn't exactly appeal to me. On the contrary, the presence of good old Mathias did not sit well with the frisky mothers and teachers in ecstasy who populated my fantasies in these moments.

"C'mon. It'll be fun."

Without waiting for me to reply, he went at it. I stared nervously at the ceiling while Mathias fidgeted under the covers a few inches away from me.

Suddenly, he stopped.

"What are you doing, Vic? Aren't you doing it?"

I didn't want to disappoint him. Or maybe it was too humiliating for him to do it all by himself. I turned on my side facing the wall and moved my arm under the covers to simulate the action that I knew so well.

After that, whenever I went to sleep over at his place, it became our ritual. At the end of the evening, Mathias would suggest that we each do it on our own. It was always the same. He would masturbate for real, and I would just pretend.

The Incident

At this point, I had become a world expert on experimental masturbology. At night I would turn off the light in my room and go to sleep peacefully, filled with the confidence of someone who never got caught.

What I didn't know was that my secret kingdom was about to collapse.

We had just finished dinner. My mother and my stepfather were doing the dishes and listening to the radio in the kitchen. After clearing the table and sweeping up, I'd gone back to my room to do my homework.

In the middle of a particularly difficult algebra problem, I suddenly felt an urgent need to take a break. At the other end of the house, I could hear music mixed with the voices of my parents and the sound of the dishes in the sink.

I went to close the door and opened my sock drawer to fetch my usual materials — Kleenex, Vaseline and the photo of Aunt Sylvie. Everything was in place for another uneventful masturbation session. I lay on my bed, pulled my jeans down to my thighs and got to work. Oddly, I was in less of a hurry than usual.

Just as I was reaching climax, I stopped and let everything subside before going back at it again. I wanted to make the pleasure last and, most of all, delay the moment when I would have to return to my math notebook.

Then, just when I was in the full swing of things, the door opened and in walked my mother with a basket of clean laundry in her arms.

In a panic, I just had time to slide the photo of my aunt Sylvie under my left butt cheek. I grabbed the pillow that was under my head and stuffed it between my legs, but it was too late. My mother had seen everything.

After a moment of hesitation that seemed to last a thousand years, she muttered apologies and left with the laundry basket still in her arms.

It was over. I was toast. The outside world was now aware that a terrible sex maniac was lurking beneath the exterior of this nice boy. Victor Number Two had been unmasked.

I put away my equipment and quickly got dressed. That night I did my math homework with unprecedented fervor and stayed in my room until every single light in the house was off.

Never in my whole life had I been so embarrassed to be me.

The next morning when I left my room, I found the basket of clothes in front of my door. When I arrived in the kitchen, my mother was in the middle of breakfast. I said hi and kept my head lowered as I went to the toaster.

I was sitting at the end of the table eating my toast and unable to speak. I had the impression that anything I said would sound like a pathetic attempt to try to cover up what had happened the day before.

Finally, while I was counting the crumbs on my plate, my mother approached. I didn't even dare look at her. I was waiting for a bad joke or, even worse, that she would want the two of us to have a "chat" about sex.

Instead, she kissed me on the top of my head and left the kitchen to go and get dressed.

That was it. Neither of us ever talked about the incident.

During the months that followed, I continued to masturbate daily. Soon, new faces replaced those of Madame Aziba and Aunt Sylvie at the top of my erotic rankings. But after that morning, something changed. With a simple gesture, my mother had made me understand that it was okay. That it was okay to be fourteen years old and that there was nothing disgusting about being a masturbation enthusiast.

Who knows? Maybe it was even totally normal.

My ~~First~~ Time
Laurence Beaudoin-Masse

My skirt slipped. When I got up from my stool at the bar, it came undone and fell down to the fleshy part of my thighs. And in its descent revealed the slim-control panel of my pantyhose and, beneath the transparent Lycra, my little white panties.

It was difficult to do up, this skirt, because of the complicated clasps. It wasn't mine. I'd stolen it. This was my first-ever date and in preparation I'd decided that none of my clothes would do. So I'd rummaged through my mother's things.

Yeah, I know. The idea that the wardrobe of a forty-year-old attorney would be more suitable for the occasion seems debatable today, but at the time, it made sense.

So, I'd stolen an old-lady skirt, and said skirt now

refused to cooperate. In figure skating we would say this was a wardrobe malfunction. In real life I would hope we wouldn't say anything at all. I would hope that no one in the bar noticed the incident. No one, starting with Adam.

So. First date ever. I'd met Adam two days before on an app. We'd exchanged photos — just the good ones — a few charming but unremarkable words, and we arranged to meet up in a bar.

He was at least eighteen, unlike me. He had already dated, unlike me. But I acted as though I had. I was good at that — faking it. Seriously allergic to the idea of not being in control of a situation, of being the beginner at anything whatsoever.

Like when my mother had wanted to explain how to put in a tampon. I'd refused to listen, offended, said I knew how to do it. Truth was that I'd been wearing the tampon *with* the applicator in my vagina until, in a stroke of genius, I realized that you used the little plastic tube to push the piece of cotton in deep — a bit like sending a rocket into space — and then removed the applicator.

In short, I was proud and stubborn. I did not give myself the right to have first times.

If I was there, dressed in a forty-year-old lawyer's skirt in a bar before even turning eighteen, it was because I was looking for love. And I'm not saying "looking for love" to be cute. No, no, no. I was looking for love the way others searched for a vaccine formula. I searched methodically, tenaciously, relentlessly. I'd seen the film. I believed love would save me. I had dedicated my high-school years to becoming infatuated with guys who, no matter what their style, size or interests, had in common the fact of not being in love with me. There was nothing that could be done about it.

So when I got to CEGEP[1], I was beyond desperate. My hope grew heavier, got bigger. It weighed me down with its big dirty hands.

That's how it happened — a dating app, the bar, the skirt with complicated clasps, Adam.

Perhaps I should also clarify that I was fat. Not just fat in my own mind. No. Objectively fat. I had been fat throughout high school — different at an age when being like everyone else is pretty much the only thing that matters. An age when you have to be like everyone else, but absolutely unique at the same time.

So, I was big. Also beautiful. Undeniably beautiful. I only realized that much later, when I looked at the photos.

Anyway. I was living a bit like I was stuck in a waiting room, uncomfortable and irritated. I was in a hurry to leave adolescence, in a hurry to be an adult, in a hurry to find my people. To find love. Because love would save me from a dull and disappointing life.

At least that's what I hoped. Really hoped.

So. Adam had arranged to meet at eight o'clock. I arrived fifteen minutes early. I was nervous. The dim

1 CEGEP: A public school that provides the first level of post-secondary education in Quebec, Canada.

lighting, the soft music, the polished wood, velvet armchairs ... I had never even been to a place like this on my own. I desperately hoped to go unnoticed, to melt into the background. That no one would question that I had a right to be here. I was indeed an adult, sure — just an adult in a body that had not yet reached the age of majority.

Fortunately, it seemed that no one cared. Partly, I thought, thanks to the skirt with the complicated clasps.

When Adam arrived, I was struck by the intensity of his cologne. It was a sharp, flowery scent, slightly cloying. His face was softer, more babyish than his photos, his head buried in his curly hair, his blue-gray eyes and blond beard. I discovered everything that was missing in his photo. The way he let his shoulders sag slightly forward, the nasal edge to his voice, the weird way he blinked ...

He was different than the picture I'd had of him, but whatever. I would accept him as he was. I was just happy that he'd turned up, that he'd chosen me.

Also relieved that he hadn't turned and run. That he was sitting down, smiling at me, offering me a drink.

Shy, I barely dared to look at him. I buried myself in the menu, which I perused nervously, overwhelmed by the list of cocktails. I ordered something or other, hoping it wouldn't taste too strong. That it wouldn't come in a tiny glass. That I wouldn't grimace when I tasted it.

Conversation was stiff and full of silences, but I was a willing participant. I put on my best performance. The question for me wasn't whether I liked Adam or was attracted to him. No. I wanted to please him. For a long time I had thought that being desirable was much more important than desiring something myself.

Adam was a student. Studying political science. That alone was exciting. That alone was a good story. I was having a drink with a political science student. I was definitely going to throw that in the face of my best friend, Jade. Jade had just scored the famous double win — "find a great love and go to the prom with him." I was jealous. She was living her best life, and I was still being forgotten by fate. I had gone to the prom alone, like dryer lint tossed in the laundry room trash can.

I was already thinking about how I would tell her the story about Adam — the important details, and the ones I would forget. I wouldn't tell her about the app, that's for sure. I would mention our animated conversation. I'd describe how I'd kissed Adam goodbye. An interesting finale to an amazing story.

I was far from imagining that the evening was about to take a completely different turn.

After one drink, I already knew that Adam and I were not headed for a great future together. That the chemistry wasn't there. I was disappointed, tired. All that wasted time, all that pointless, wasted momentum. And that's probably one reason why I didn't see it coming when, after a long stretch of silence, Adam invited me to his room for a last drink. His residence room at the university.

I said yes without thinking about it too much, without even giving myself time to breathe.

I knew what that meant — "for a last drink." That was code for "sleep together." While I'd neglected to learn how to make a martini, I had already mastered several adult life conventions. How to say "I'm well, thanks," when asked "How are you?" or categorically refuse when a guest offered to do the dishes, even when they insisted.

I'll admit that the prospect of a "sexuality" project with Adam hadn't crossed my mind, not even for two seconds. I was there to look for love and maybe even find it. That was the plan, the first step.

Except that sitting in the bar, the idea of refusing his invitation seemed absurd. I'd come, I'd ordered a drink, chatted. I was going to follow his lead. He wanted more than a casual banal conversation in a cozy bar, so I was going to give him more. *I'll go where you go, Adam.*

That's what grown-ups did, right? None of this "take your time," "wait until you're ready" or, the worst — "wait until the right person comes along."

I stood up. And it was at precisely that moment when my skirt slipped down my thighs. As I pulled it up and tucked the top into my tights, I decided that this would be the first time. My first sexual relationship. I found this to be extremely embarrassing information. I had to keep it to myself at all costs.

Walking to the residence in the bittersweet October air, I took a discreet inventory of my previous almost or quasi-sexual experiences. I didn't want to overlook anything. I was going to need all the practical knowledge at my disposal. I wanted Adam to think that I'd already done it. That was very important. And if things went well, I would lose my virginity as a bonus, and that idea pleased me. I didn't want to make love, no, but I certainly wanted to have done it.

I quickly reviewed my memories. I had already kissed a neighbor the summer I was fifteen. Nicolas. I had a huge crush on him.

The first two minutes had been incredible. A dazzling French kiss that left me stunned. Sitting on his bed in front of an unfinished game of *Mario Kart*, I was floating, lovesick, ready to declare my devotion to him, confess my feelings. But I had no time to speak before he'd taken my hand and put it on his penis.

Apart from noting that his penis was throbbing beneath his pants, I'd done nothing. I was frozen.

In the days that followed, I saw Nicolas several times to watch movies, but found myself faced with the same issue each time. Two minutes of fantastic kissing before my hand was kidnapped and resting inert on his erect penis. That could last a long time — the length of a feature film, at least. I wasn't going to move my hand, and I wasn't going to take it away.

Because at the beginning of the summer, to make myself sound interesting, I'd told him that I had already "done stuff." Of course it was a lie — a big lie, the kind of thing that just slipped out. But ever since then, I think he was very, very impatient that I would "do stuff" to him, too. Which I, myself, had absolutely no desire to do.

And that was it. End of practical experience.

Adam opened the main door of the student residence, and as I rushed into the building that smelled of bacon and damp, I thought, too bad. I would have to be inspired by knowledge freely available on the internet.

Because, like everyone else, I had already watched porn.

I expected a lot of things when I walked into Adam's little room, but I didn't really expect to get one last drink. He served me a tiny glass of some syrupy yellow drink that he took straight out of the mini freezer of his mini fridge. Something sent from Europe by his parents — limoncello, I think.

I was sitting on his bed and waiting. The connection between us was not particularly obvious. I had long since exhausted the list of possible conversation topics. I was wondering how to raise the "sexuality" project as precious minutes ticked by without him or me making the first move. Time marched on with big, heavy feet, with me sinking into the bed, more and more passive, my limbs limp.

He had put on some music. Uninteresting music. The chances of a spontaneous rapprochement were melting away in the hot air of the residence like the ice in my glass. I did nothing. I was a lump of exhaustion, of unbearable passivity.

Embarrassed, I finally got up to put down my empty glass and maybe leave. Strategic withdrawal. I'd say something like, Thank you for the nice evening, and then go. It would be much better that way.

I put my ridiculous little glass on the corner of a ridiculous little table, and Adam quickly stood up to give me a ridiculous little kiss on the corner of my mouth.

I kissed him back. We had to start somewhere.

First off, foreplay. Wet tongue, rough skin, cold fingertips. Sensations more strange than pleasant. Lying on top of me, Adam did his best, giving generously of his hands, his mouth, his pelvis. So much so that his belt buckle dug into the flesh of my stomach, bruising it and preventing me from appreciating the effort. I tried to take it off by pulling, and he leaned back to help me, as well as undoing his jeans.

Our gazes crossed. Right away I pulled him to me to kiss him again. When we kissed, we didn't have to look at each other. Then I made the mistake of sliding my tongue along his neck.

The burn of cologne. The taste of a thousand garish flowers burst in my mouth. I produced as much saliva as possible and bravely swallowed to get rid of the awful taste. I was convinced that a more experienced partner would not have made the same mistake. As if this was another convention of adult life. Never kiss a perfumed person on the neck. I took note.

We were going to have to undress. This was the step I

feared the most. No one had ever seen me naked, except maybe my sister. Sitting on the bed was easy. I slid off my skirt, unhooked my bra, pulled off my tights. Kept on my white panties. White panties ... If I had thought I was going to be showing them to anyone that evening, I would have chosen black.

Then, practically naked, I held my breath nervously. Waiting for the next step.

He made a comment about my breasts. I will never forget it. They're big, yes, but one is smaller than the other. He showed me which one, amused. I found this petty. Adam, that is, not my big little breast. I knew his comment would always be the first thing that the first man to see me naked had said. I was disappointed, but I didn't let it show. He removed my panties, slid a finger in my vagina. I felt nothing. I touched his penis, trying to imitate the movements I'd seen on the internet.

Until that moment, I had thought very little about the texture of the thing. Sex involves a lot more textures than I'd been prepared for. The penis stunned me. Hard but spongy. Solid but not. Smooth, so smooth. And a bit slimy.

Then the clothes, the skin, the saliva, the sheets, the sweat, the hair, the mucus, the bumps on the tongue. I was assailed with textures, impressions, substances like so many micro-invasions.

I stayed the course. But in spite of all my efforts, my hand would do nothing but mechanically rub Adam's penis. I searched for the right level of pressure without finding it, without daring to ask. I stroked him without knowing whether it was giving him pleasure. The theoretical courses were useless. It was time to quickly move on to the next stage. My plan was foolproof.

I grabbed the condom, unwrapped it, put it on him and finally let Adam penetrate me.

No sensation. Nothing. Adam came and went inside me without arousing me. I instinctively began to make little noises. A soundtrack for our romp in the hay. I sent groans of pleasure into his ear. Why, I don't know. I was not feeling ecstasy, no. But I played my part. And even if I already knew how fake pornography was, how misleading, I was in shock. The bodies, the organs, the positions, the duration, the scenarios ... I'd been warned they were false, retouched, invented.

What I didn't know was that they also exaggerated the pleasure. I thought that being penetrated meant I would feel pleasure. That it was automatic, inevitable.

But no matter how hard I tried or concentrated, I felt nothing. At all. My first time was nothing but textures and friction.

What a disappointment. What a waste of time, again.

I did not panic. I waited. Clinging to my partner's back, I let him do it. For a long time. For me it became uncomfortable, but he seemed to like it. That was the most important thing, no?

"Do you want to stop?" He asked the question after a

while. Vaginal dryness. My body had betrayed my secret. It was not complicit in the deceit, it did not pretend. Vaginal dryness.

I should have said, *Yes, I prefer to stop.* But I didn't, no. I wet my fingers with saliva, I denied, I persevered.

I've already said I was proud. And I wasn't going to tell Jade a story that ended like this. That ended with a forfeit, with abandonment. It was out of the question. I'd come into the residence, I'd had a drink, given up my virginity, and I was going to see it through.

And that's exactly what I did. It's perhaps my biggest regret, not to have stopped, set my limit.

Then Adam ejaculated, and at last it was over.

Sex is often disappointing, that's normal. On the other hand, I wish someone had told me that desire is not negotiable. That experiencing it isn't just important, it's essential.

After getting rid of the condom, Adam offered to pay for my taxi. I found his proposal inappropriate. The idea that he could pay me whatever was inappropriate.

I put my skirt back on and left for the metro. Swallowing my pride. Swallowing my shame. He texted me a few days later. Just to suggest that we see each other again. I was astonished. I didn't reply.

I told Jade a story delicately edited, romanticized, a bit spicy. I minimized the extent of my disillusionment. Magnified the sensations, the pleasure. I certainly wasn't going to talk about my first time as a failure, an empty sadness. Out of the question. I made like it was of no importance to me in any case.

I knew she would see through me. That she would tell me that I should have leaned on her, shared my disappointment. Laughed about my questionable decisions with her.

Because, really, what is the point of making mistakes, if not to at least be consoled in the arms of someone you love?

My Chouchounette, My Faith and Me

Schelby Jean-Baptiste

INNOCENCE

I must have been twelve or thirteen years old the first time I started to think about sex. In my self-conscious young teenaged mind the simple act of kissing or touching a person was the same as losing one's virginity.

Only later did I understand that what I was really afraid of was losing my innocence. A glance. A touch. A kiss. A penetration.

It took a long time for me to realize there were many steps before the ultimate step — The First Time.

And I especially realized something else. That the first

time isn't just sex with penetration. No. There are other ways to make love.

I'm thinking about the first time I made love with ... myself.

But before I really dive in to this subject, I want to introduce you to the one who knows and understands me the best. My Chouchounette.

Chouchounette.

I think it sounds sweet, thoughtful, funny and awkward all at the same time. And all those words still ring true today when it comes to describing my first sexual experience. I never would have thought that Chouchounette and I would have such powerful and intimate moments together.

So, getting back to my epic journey.

DUALITY

I'm seventeen years old. I consider myself Québécoise, but my background is Haitian. Most children of immigrants will understand why this information is important to this story. There are many similarities in the way we have been brought up.

So, I'm seventeen and I live with my parents. I am Christian — Protestant, to be exact. According to the state, I'm almost an adult. But at my house, I'm still a child. So intimacy and privacy are not part of my life. This situation creates a strange kind of tension. On the one hand, the desire to make love to myself is starting to cross my mind more and more. On the other hand, the suffocating presence of my parents hampers this need that is begging to be explored.

That said, I haven't always felt this desire.

It's when I arrive at the school of freedom — also known as CEGEP — that I learn about female masturbation.

"Wait, what? Women can masturbate? That's disgusting! What kind of woman engages in this kind of sexual activity? Surely not good girls!"

That's what I think. My mind cannot accept the idea that a woman can be a good person and sexually free at the same time.

Sad? Truly. But this was the way I looked at life at the time.

A heated discussion on the subject breaks out between one of my friends and me. My arguments spurt out like lava from a volcano as I try to make my friend understand that masturbation for women is sexual perversion, and that sex is only acceptable and respectable after marriage. She laughs in my face and argues that sexuality is normal and even healthy and that a woman should know her own body instead of asking a man to do it for her.

"It gives way too much power to someone who will never know you better than you know yourself," she says.

"Only men can have pleasure when it comes to sex," I reply quickly.

"Oh, come on! Have you ever masturbated?"

"Agh, no!"

"Oh, God! Get out of your closed-mindedness and live a little! It won't hurt you!"

In the moment I have nothing to say in my defense. The conversation gets heated. I try to think about a verse from the Bible that I can throw in her face, but nothing comes to mind. I realize that what she's saying is true, but I can't get it into my young virginal Christian head that's been so steeped in religious ideals.

It's important for me to be clear about something: I have nothing against religion. Many wonderful values that I hold today come courtesy of religion. That said, religion has stunted my imagination, and my sexuality.

Part of me wants to go out and discover the unknown. Live a little, like my friend says. A curious little voice is whispering to me and singing in my ear her desire to explore the most mysterious parts of my body. And this little voice starts to take up more and more space.

I am extremely torn. I don't understand why God made me with so many contradictions. Why pit me against myself? Why wasn't I born without desire? Without needs? Without a vagina! The questions go on and soon I have trouble sleeping. I am really trying to understand life, and let me tell you, it's not super easy. I feel like I'm the only one in the world with this problem. I can't talk about too much with my sister, because I'm afraid of disappointing her and not being seen as proper and perfect. And this isn't the kind of discussion I see myself having with my mother, since she's never given me any guidance about sexual matters.

It's complicated ...

The more time passes, the more my desire to meet my Chouchounette excites me and occupies my thoughts. I tell myself that if I'm not in control of the situation, Chouchounette will control me. And I *absolutely* do not want that to happen.

Attack mode: On.

But I have to find a way to make love to myself with the utmost subtlety.

Easy enough, you say? Uh ... no. Truly not. This is going to be one of the biggest challenges of my short life. How to make sure that no one comes into the room that I share with my sister at that very moment? I remind you that I live in a house with a *Haitian family*. Every possible catastrophic scenario crosses my mind.

IMAGINED SCENARIO

CUT TO:

A soft light caresses Schelby's still emerging curves. She gently touches her neck, her breasts, her belly, quietly moving down to the royal kingdom. The place where the angels and her ancestors are waiting to celebrate the greatest victory — the liberation of her Chouchounette.

Oh, what a great day this will be!

Suddenly, a herd consisting of her parents, her

brothers, her grandmother and her sister walk into the room.

MY MOTHER: OH! JESUS!

MY GRANDMOTHER: WHAT'S GOING ON HERE?

MAIN CHARACTER (traumatized but still quite lucid, in her head): I believe it's quite clear what's going on.

(Out loud): NOTHING! I WAS FEELING THE BOTTOM SHEET TO SEE IF IT WAS AS SOFT AS I THOUGHT IT WAS!

Wait. What?

End of sketchy scenario.

Yeah, I'm not a very good liar. Being caught in the act is really the last thing that should happen to me.

DISCOVERY — FIRST TRY

It's the big day. My first date with myself. My first encounter with Chouchounette.

I'm feeling a mix of anxiety and excitement.

It's a rainy fall day. Leaves the color of fire are carried away by the wind and end up lying on the wet pavement.

Above them, raindrops hit my bedroom window — sometimes quietly, sometimes frenetically.

I'm at home. In my underwear. Under a big blanket.

My bedroom light is off to create a mysterious and sensual atmosphere.

The candles are lit.

Simple but dramatic.

I am ready to experience my first masturbation.

Suddenly, a very uncomfortable heat takes over my body.

I am *hotttt*.

A bit too hot. I go to lift off the blanket, but the idea that someone might open the door and burst in out of nowhere stops me.

I freeze.

But the heat doesn't stop.

It's getting hotter and *hotter*!

I am suddenly super embarrassed.

About who? About what?

About myself.

I am overwhelmed by shame.

I feel like I'm being watched.

I'm alone but I feel like the Kingdom of God is watching me. The angels, the spirits ... *Jesus!* Everyone is here! I'm afraid to come out from under the covers to get dressed, because I don't want them to judge me, even if I know perfectly well that they already know exactly what's going on.

A mountain of questions fills my head.

Where is all this desire coming from? Am I falling straight into hell? Is that why it's so hot? Is it normal for my body to react like this? Am I possessed by the devil? Should I talk about it?

The truth is that I would like to be able to keep this moment of desire to myself, in my little secret garden.

What should I do?

I'm trying to concentrate, but all I can hear is the rain tapping gently on the window.

I pay attention to the sound.

Tap. Tap. Tap. Tap.

The sound makes me feel good. I start to imagine myself out walking in the rain. I've always loved the rain. It reminds me that there are bigger things than us. Nature never ceases to amaze me.

The rain calms me down.

The rain allows me to stop thinking about anything.

Then. The rain brings me back to reality. I am alone in my room for an indefinite time, without knowing at which exact moment my family will arrive.

I can't relax.

I seriously start to wonder what's wrong with me.

It's like I'm about to have a bad trip, even though I haven't smoked or taken drugs.

Things are not going well.

I need to change the atmosphere, calm down. Maybe that will set up a better experience with Chouchounette.

She deserves it. I deserve it. That's what I keep telling myself.

I touch my semi-naked body with the tips of my fingers under the covers. This is all really new to me. Normally I am only naked when I'm in the shower.

The shower!!!

Boom! I have an idea.

I remember a conversation I had with my friends. They said that one of their tricks was to spray their Chouchounette with water from the showerhead.

Ah! That's it! I have renewed hope for the whole adventure.

I need to get in the shower! That's the solution. Maybe that's why the sound of the rain feels so good.

I spring out of bed and look around for a towel.

I find one! Yes!

Except ...

It's there on the chest of drawers beside the door, but it's beneath a pile of *church* clothes! Skirts, blouses, long dresses. And let's not forget the Bible, which is sitting not far away.

I start to question myself *again*. Is this a message from God? Why is the towel lying under the church clothes? Did I put them there as a subconscious reminder that everything lying beneath the church is bad?

Agh, no! Goddammit! I'm starting to go in circles.

Standing there with my breasts exposed, I try to think. I don't know what to do.

I have to pray.

I get down on my knees in front of the pile of clothes and the towel.

"Dear Jesus, I know I'm not supposed to be completely naked in your presence right now, and I apologize, but I need some clarification here. I decided to come before you like this because I am in my most vulnerable state. My body wants to have a sexual experience, but I keep receiving signs that tell me I shouldn't do it. I want to know if these are really signs or if I'm overthinking it. I need a response from you. Why am I feeling sexual desires, but at the same time I feel like I am sinning? I am really starting to find it difficult to live a human life."

While I recite this prayer, tears start to run down my face.

I'm filled with a feeling of extreme confusion.

I feel paralyzed in this body. In this world. In this life.

I have a knot in my stomach. A hole in my heart.

It's all too much for me.

I want to cry.

I cry.

I want to scream.

I scream.

I want to get up.

I can't.

My body suddenly becomes super heavy.

I lie in a little ball on the floor and continue to cry.

Black out.

I hear the sound of *honking*.

I startle.

I'm on the ground.

Lying down. Half-naked.

God damn it! Time has passed and I must have fallen asleep.

The honking continues.

I grab my church clothes and rush to where the noise is coming from.

I look out the window.

It's my mother. She's leaning on the horn signaling to my sister to get out of the way.

My sister, who is rummaging around in her bag, turns and heads toward the front door.

Jesus Christ! I have to get dressed!

I quickly start to pull on my clothes.

I hear the sound of the key in the lock. I finish putting on my sweater.

My sister walks in the house. She comes up the stairs. I hear her steps coming closer and closer. She's about to open the door.

I haven't had time to put on my skirt.

This is it. I am going to be exposed.

Never again will she look at me as her little sister, but like a little lapsed pervert.

She opens the door. I close my eyes.

Then suddenly …

Nothing.

Her nose buried in her cell phone, she quickly says hi, dumps her things in the room and leaves.

"That's it?" I ask myself.

I take a deep breath and burst out laughing.

Okay, so my masturbation plan won't happen this time.

DISCOVERY — TAKE TWO

As I expected, no one is home today. Still, I make sure to lock the front door. Then I remember that everyone in my family has a house key, and they could come home at any moment. I block the door with a chair. But then I start to have doubts. This scenario could lead my family to believe that I've been kidnapped and barricaded in the house.

Result? Twenty police cars waiting for me outside.

Inhale. Exhale. Inhale. Exhale.

That's what you'd tell me to do, isn't it?

No time.

I remove the chair and tell myself that God will watch over me. I see him like my buddy. And buddies, I tell myself, understand your needs.

I go into the bathroom.

I watch myself in the mirror as I get undressed. Did you know it's good for your self-esteem to look at yourself naked? Yup, I know. *Awkward!* Anyway, even if it's horribly embarrassing, I admire myself. My God, I find myself beautiful and sexy. Wow!

Okay, good, a little concentration. I head to the shower.

I turn on the water and make sure it's the right temperature. Then I get in. I really like this. I think I have a true affinity with water.

Before long, I'm standing under the hot water.

I am absolutely positive that no one is at home. It's a day off at CEGEP, my grandmother has gone to church, and my sister and my parents are working. DAMMMMN! It's a party in my head!

As the water runs down my body, I remember how my friends told me not to be afraid to use the hand shower.

But it's hard to use a non-removable showerhead. So I take a little bucket and fill it with water. I pour it over my lower belly. Hmmm ... the water runs over my Chouchounette way too fast. I'm not feeling it much. I'm actually uncomfortable.

I'm starting to get the feeling that discovering one's sexuality might be synonymous with discomfort.

Yup. That's the word: discomfort.

I try to figure out how to get out of this uncomfortable situation.

Think. Think. Think.

Trey Songz! *Yesss!*

*

When I was a teenager, my absolute biggest crush was the R&B singer Trey Songz. I was totally hot for him. I even made an album with photos of him on my Facebook page. (I know what you're thinking, so don't bother trying to find it. I deleted the album.)

I'll never forget that first time I saw him live. He was opening for Usher in 2010 at the Bell Centre. I was with my best friend and I'd brought a red bra with my number written on it. The idea was that he would catch it and call me during his stay in Montreal. In my head, he was staying for a week after the show.

I had the whole thing figured out. What I hadn't thought through, however, was that I could have sent him straight to prison. I was seventeen, and he was twenty-six! Clearly at that age I understood nothing about life!

Finally, I gave up on my plan — not because of our age gap but because there were sketchy-looking guys standing in front of us and I was afraid they'd grab my bra. I would end up having to change my number!

*

Okay. Back to reality.

I'm thinking about Trey Songz. I turn off the water, dry myself quickly with the towel, then wrap it around me. I run to my room because I'm *cold!* I grab my CD player, my Trey Songz CD and return to the bathroom.

I make sure I'm nice and dry before I plug in the CD player. It's all about the details. It would be too bad if I electrocuted myself before my first orgasm.

"She was so young and in love with life. Her last moments of pleasure were abruptly interrupted just as she was about to come. So tragic!"

I put on the first song of the *Ready* album. "Panty Droppa" is on! *Damm!* I'm already feeling more into it. I imagine that Trey Songz is waiting for me in the bath.

I'm excited at the idea of opening the shower curtain and finding him on the other side.

I turn off the light and get into the shower.

Of course, *absolutely no one* is waiting for me. No problem. Trey's voice is right here with me.

I feel it. It's going to happen.

I can't believe I'm actually home alone. Everything has been planned out. I have at least two hours before my grandmother arrives from church. Surely enough time to make myself come.

Because, yes, in my little young-adult head, I'm sure I will have an orgasm right away. Hahaha!

But, nothing.

Nada.

Silence. My Chouchounette is not talking to me. She's embarrassed.

Drier than you could imagine.

My Chouchounette is not receptive. Not at all.

I don't understand. I have done everything to make my plan work. The lights are out, Trey Songz is gently playing in the background. My Chouchounette is fresh and ready for some love. I'm trying to understand what she wants.

Nothing.

Total disappointment. I start to panic. What if my Chouchounette is broken?

I've never asked myself this question, and it's not the kind of conversation I want to have with my friends or the people at church.

I start to cry. I feel defeated. Useless. Alone.

It's not possible! Every time I want to do something good for myself, I end up in tears. Is this normal?

I feel let down, but because I've always been a person who tries to find solutions for everything, I promise Chouchounette that I will fix her.

I tell myself that maybe I shouldn't be thinking about Trey Songz, given the corruption-of-a-minor situation.

My thoughts go in another direction.

I close my eyes, let the water run and call my imagination to the rescue.

A big beautiful hand the color of cocoa caresses my neck, my chest, then quietly moves lower. He must be about seventeen. I don't even have time to react before his beautiful big luscious lips press against mine. They are soft and hungry at the same time.

In spite of the awkwardness of it all, Chouchounette, amazingly enough, likes it, and so does he. I says "he" because I get the impression it's a male, but I don't see his face or his features. He's blurry. Almost nonexistent.

On the other hand, I feel him. Oh, yeah, I feel himmmmm! If you know what I mean? Ha! I feel him *verrrry* well. His presence makes my whole body vibrate and awakens desires that have been hiding inside my body. I would like to pray for clarity, but I also want to stay in the present moment.

I am almost there. I am ready to see his magnificent face. My Chouchounette is truly aroused. She's awake!

She's awake! I have never felt like this before. My eyes are still closed, I see the young man retreating into a beautiful light. It's an angel! I tell myself that it must be an angel. A slightly naughty angel, but still, better than a demon.

Chouchounette is at the peak of excitement, and I focus to make out the features of my imaginary lover...

Suddenly, a familiar voice.

"Schelby! You're wasting all the hot water. I need to use the bathroom!"

Wow! It's my grandmother!

I pull myself out of my fantasy. I open my eyes wide.

What is she doing here?

She explains that she wasn't feeling well and asked a Sister at the church to bring her back home.

God damn it!

I turn the tap to C and spray my Chouchounette with cold water to calm her down.

I turn off the water, take the towel and run to my room so my grandmother can sit on the toilet.

When I go into my room, I catch my gaze in the mirror. I smile.

I smile, because even if I didn't succeed in having an orgasm, I did feel something.

TRUTH

The truth is that getting to know myself has embarrassed, traumatized and haunted me for a long time.

Even today, I'm not a pro. I don't always know how to go about it. My body doesn't always want to cooperate. For a long time this has been a hard pill to swallow, because there was a time when I sincerely wanted to be able to tell my friends that I, too, was capable of making myself come. That I, too, was in tune with myself.

In a society where sexuality rules, it's easy to feel like you're not up to standard. Later, you wonder whether others have also struggled and are just pretending.

In the end, life works out. Always. I've met several older women who have nothing left to prove as far as their sexuality goes, and who have been kind and generous enough to share their personal sexual experiences with me.

They blew my mind.

Among other things, they reassured me that discovering your sexuality isn't a race, but a long and above all pleasant process.

Damn!!!

Their advice still resonates with me. Strong. Quick. Sometimes in slow motion. Often.

So I am exactly where I should be, and happy to know that Chouchounette is never far away.

The Sad Story of My Virginity

Pierre-Yves Villeneuve

"Apparently it wasn't suicide," Seb tells me as we walk to the dépanneur. "Looks like he was murdered."

"Are you serious?"

Kurt Cobain died three days ago. It's impossible to ignore. When the news broke, it was all anybody talked about — between classes, in the cafeteria, waiting for the bus. The shock wave was enormous.

"Wait a minute. Why would anyone kill Kurt Cobain? That doesn't make any sense!"

Sébastien has no answer. We knew Cobain was a handful, and the powers that be don't like anyone who rattles the cage too much. You're allowed to disrupt the established order, but only if someone can make a profit from it. My friend frowns and shrugs his shoulders, as if the senselessness alone of the Nirvana singer's death justifies this theory.

The flaw with Seb's hypothesis is that it's impossible to prove. To find out what really happened, you'd have to let the journalists investigate, which takes time. But if no one quickly confirms the murder theory, the people responsible for his death could throw out 427 more "plausible" versions that will end up burying the truth forever.

The store is at the corner of Saint-Martin and De la Mauricie. I have a pretty convincing fake ID, but it would be stupid to get caught and have to go to the party empty-handed, given that Seb is an adult. So I let him go in and buy a six-pack of Black Label while I wait outside.

Beginning of April. The snow hasn't finished melting. It's still cold, but not too cold. I'm shivering. I could do up my coat, but I haven't done that all winter, and I'm not going to start tonight. I just stick my hands in my pockets, where I've stashed two novels — one by Isaac Asimov in the left and one by Arthur C. Clarke in the right. I always have at least one book on me, usually more.

"Let's go, Pouaye!" Seb shouts triumphantly, coming out of the store.

There are piles of gravel along the curb, so we walk right down the middle of the street and talk. I tell him about an astronomy book I got from the library, and he tells me about the last Bois-de-Boulogne CEGEP party where he got with some girl. They snuck off the dance floor and hid out in an elevator. Seb remains vague. He doesn't need to get into the juicy details. Just the idea of a girl turns me on.

Shit. I pull my coat tight around me so nothing shows.

Seb has always had more success with girls than me. I wish I was easygoing and jokey, could talk to girls like him. I'm kind of a shy type. Kind of very shy. Everyone knows girls prefer rowdy guys, and I'm just a nice guy who's a good listener.

Ugh! Me and the good listeners, we're all going to die virgins.

At seventeen, I'm hoping I can still get a real first girlfriend. I've already kissed a girl or two, but there's a difference between kissing a girl with ketchup and hotdog breath when you're playing spin the bottle at the end of elementary school and really kissing a girl. The number of times it's happened seems more like a margin of error than something I can brag about. I have a hard time imagining the day when a girl is going to be interested in me — even less one when I'll get to sleep with her.

"So?"

"So what?"

He stops in the middle of the street and looks at me as if it's obvious. Fuck. I missed part of the conversation. I had to be on the moon or dreaming of Mars or Phobos. I have no idea what Seb is talking about.

"Have you ever been sucked off?"

What? We weren't talking about me. Why is he asking me this?

Without blinking, I lie.

"Sure."

Perfectly natural tone, without emphasis, nice and casual. Fake it till you make it. Anyone could swear it's the truth and nothing but the truth. But Sébastien isn't just anyone. He's been my best friend for a long time. We know each other too well. He gives me a close look and smirks a little and shakes his head. He knows I'm lying. I know he knows, but I keep going.

"Well, yeah, Seb."

Infallible, concrete argument. Well, yeah. I love astrophysics and sci-fi, but if ever those don't work out, I could become a lawyer tomorrow morning, given my legendary powers of oratory.

"How was it?"

Goddammit!

"Um, well, you know. It's ... hard to describe, but, well ..." I'm dodging, shrugging my shoulders. "It was, uh ... sweet?"

I am so stupid. I should have kept my mouth shut. For starters, my answer sounds more like a question, like I'm waiting for him to confirm it. And such a dumb answer (boring and lacking imagination!) makes it obvious that I'm lying.

I know he already knows that and that he knows I know, but appearance counts. That's what matters.

"And who was the lucky girl?" he presses.

"Oh, come on, Seb! I'm not going to tell you her name because let's say you blab and it gets out, it wouldn't be cool for her. You know?"

What a pathetic excuse! Seb laughs and grabs me by the neck. I elbow him in the ribs. We jockey back and forth down the street, careful not to damage our precious cargo.

A few more blocks and we arrive at the party house. Vicky, Geneviève and Nicolas are on the porch having a smoke. None of them have bothered to put on their coats. Seb and I go in and immediately head for the basement, where there must easily be about thirty people. Twenty or so from Mont-Saint-Louis and a dozen strangers. Strangers to me, that is. Someone here must know them. They must go to another school — Horizon, or Laval College or something like that.

I spot some friends, people I know. Some of them are standing around with bottles of beer in their hands. Others are spread out on a couch at the back of the room, bottles between their thighs, and a small group is sitting in a circle on the floor but they're not playing spin the bottle. A small CD player is cranking out music. Rock, mostly. Nirvana (of course), Metallica (the Black Album), Pearl Jam, all mixed in with Beastie Boys and The Clash.

Seb hands me a beer and then disappears. I join the first group where I recognize some people from my class — JF and Geneviève, to be precise. We greet each other with a little nod. They're in the middle of an animated discussion but I have no clue what they're talking about, so I just bob my head as if I do. I listen closely, trying to get a hint, take a sip of beer so I have something to do with my hands and stare at Geneviève. With her long black hair and dark eyes, she's really pretty. Naturally sexy. Not only that, but every time she talks, she licks her lips.

After a few minutes of understanding nothing of what they're talking about, I quietly slip away and go to the garage, where a bunch of metalheads are gathered.

Julien and Marc-André have brought their guitars and amps. Seb is there, sitting behind the drums, because of course. They start to play "Enter Sandman." It's loud. It's cool. *They're* cool. That's the rule. If you play an instrument, preferably an electric guitar, you're cool. More than if you're just good at science, say.

Argh. Jesus, I'm such a loser.

After a couple of songs, I go back to the other room to see if the couch is free. No luck. Annie waves at me and I join the small gang sitting on the floor.

That's when I notice her, sitting across from me.

A girl says something in her ear and she laughs as she runs her hand through her hair. Time slows down like we're in a shampoo commercial. I no longer hear the music or the noise or the tangled conversations. There's nothing but her laugh. When she smiles, two little dimples appear on her cheeks, making her even cuter. She's not wearing makeup. She doesn't need to. Her long brown hair shines between her fingers and falls back over her shoulders. She's a bit far away for me to smell her, but I'm sure she's wearing a fruity perfume that smells kind of like peaches or pears.

Shit, I'm staring at her like a big dickhead! What is the matter with me?

"I'm Catherine," she says, leaning toward me.

Time finds its rhythm again.

"What?"

I pull myself together and introduce myself, and we start to talk. With the music shaking the floor, and with friends sitting around us, the conversation is disjointed, coming from many directions at once. We jump from one subject to another, like a patchwork of sentences. When (finally) Annie gets up to go to the bathroom, I take the opportunity to move closer to Catherine. She slides a hip toward me. Soon we're sitting close enough that our knees are touching. I offer her one of my beers, which she accepts.

Catherine must have noticed the book I've been carrying around.

"Are you reading something right now?" she asks.

My golden opportunity! I go for it.

"You know Asimov? He wrote about robots and a thousand other things, too, but anyway, right now I'm reading his robot series. It's brilliant! Did you know that he's the one who invented the laws of robotics? It's crazy, because he created them at a time when there weren't even computers!"

Normally when I start talking about robots, or solar sails, or the infinitesimally small but still statistically possible chance that we'll discover an exoplanet, that's when everything goes sideways, where the girl completely loses interest, gets up and goes back to her friends and then tries to avoid me for the rest of the evening. But Catherine listens to me with a big smile, without showing the slightest sign of boredom.

I feel … actually, I have no idea what I'm feeling, because I have never experienced anything like this before. Something huge has happened, and I like it.

Catherine and I move a little closer to each other. Her face is only inches away from mine. I can smell the beer on her breath. If I leaned forward a bit, our lips would touch. Seriously, I have no idea what she's saying to me, because the only thought in my head is how much I want to kiss her. But I can't do it. There are too many people in the basement. If only they would all go away and leave us alone, it would be so much simpler!

Argh!

I look at the clock. Shit! The evening is going by too quickly. In a half hour, Seb's father is going to come to get us. I have zero desire to leave. I would give up all my novels to spend the night talking to Catherine.

Okay, okay, okay. It's now or never. I have to make up my mind or I will regret it.

Okay, go!

I'm going for it.

"Cath?" a girl calls from the stairs. "Cath, we need you!"

Shit. Sounds important. And of course this had to happen now. I feel Catherine grimacing slightly. She doesn't want to move, but she signals to the girl that she's heard her.

"I'll be right back," she says to me before going up to the main floor.

I have to find Seb. Have to talk to him. I've barely seen him all evening. He isn't in the garage or in the basement. I climb the stairs and see Catherine in the middle of consoling a girl who was sitting with us a bit earlier. She's drunk, weeping so loud you'd think someone just told her she had to have the toenails of her left foot pulled out and that they'll never grow back. Catherine signals to me that she's taking care of the situation, but that it might take a while.

I carry on and find Seb outside by the garage door without a T-shirt when the temperature has decided to go below freezing overnight. He's totally wasted. He sure didn't get in this state with our few Black Labels. Nicolas tries to grab him by the arm and make him go inside, but Seb resists. He's a basket case.

"He's been mouthing off for ten minutes," Nicolas groans.

"Okay. I'll take care of it. Let me talk to him. Yo, Seb! What are you doing?"

My friend stops moving. Frozen in the driveway, he

stares up at the few stars bright enough to appear in the sky above Laval.

"So, did you kiss her?" he asks without looking at me.

"I was about to, but you're ruining my plans. You need to go back in. It's freezing out."

"Not cold!"

"Well, I'm freezing my ass off out here."

It doesn't take more than that to convince him.

"Oh, okay, then," he says and follows me inside.

On the porch, I run into Catherine who is helping her friend put on her coat. My heart sinks when I see that she's getting ready to leave. The party is over. I didn't even realize that most people have already left.

"We have to go. She's not feeling well," she tells me.

"Yeah, I get it. We have to go soon, too."

We look into each other's eyes. I should say something, but I don't know what. I'm searching for my words, I'm about to speak, but nothing comes out. It's like there are no words right or powerful enough to describe what I want to say to her.

Catherine comes over to me. She stands on her tiptoes and kisses me on the cheek. The corners of our lips touch. Before disappearing, she slips a piece of paper into my hand. A piece of paper on which she's written the seven digits of her phone number.

"Man, too cool," Seb says, congratulating me. He's found his T-shirt.

"When should I call her?"

"I don't know," he says in a slurred voice, his eyes closed, his head nodding. "Tomorrow? This week? This week. The important thing is really to …"

"To …?"

But Seb's wise words are lost in an ethanol-fueled sleep. He's sleeping standing up. Amazingly, when his father comes to pick us up five minutes later, a simple nudge pulls him out of it and he's suddenly in top shape. Well, almost.

Sitting in the back seat, I think back on my evening, about Catherine, about everything we said to each other, about what I would have done differently. I so should have kissed her. I look at her number, learn it by heart, slide it into my jeans pocket so I don't lose it, check that's it's still there two minutes later. It is. Oof!

It takes over a week before I call her — three days to track down one of her friends at school to confirm that I wasn't dreaming and that it isn't a joke ("Yes, Pierre-Yves! I talked to Cath yesterday and she's waiting for you to call. Grow some balls before she changes her mind!") and four more before I get up the courage to dial her number. A week in which I see Catherine in my breakfast toast, hear nothing the teachers say, barely read a page of Asimov because I see her between every line. A week where I wake up with deadly erections, because I've been dreaming about her all night long.

"Hello?"

It's her! My heart is beating two hundred bpm. My pulse echoes in my ears.

"Catherine? It's Pouaye ... uh, Pierre-Yves. Hi."

"Hi. I'm glad you called." I can hear the smile in her voice.

"I wanted to call before but, um, anyway. Me too, I'm glad."

For a moment we listen to each other breathe. Then we both start to talk at the same time. We interrupt each other. We laugh, embarrassed.

"Go on."

"No, you first!" I insist.

"It was fun talking to you at the party."

I laugh.

"What?"

"I was going to say the same thing."

"Really?"

"Yeah, really. I swear. Uh, Catherine, I was wondering if ... if you might want to come over to my place on the weekend. My mom won't be here. We could watch a movie, like, if you want. Or something else."

There's silence on the line. I feel about as brave as a baby seal. Besides, I probably waited too long to call her. She's going to say no, that's for sure.

"Around one on Saturday?" she finally says.

Her reply is like a shot of adrenaline straight into my vein. I hang up with a light heart. My morale has never been higher. I am full of energy and smiling at nothing. All this for a girl I met a week ago.

"It's weird," I confess to Sébastien on the phone.

"Cupid finally strikes!" he says happily.

"What are you talking about?"

"You didn't see yourself looking at her. It was so obvious that you fell for her. An arrow to the heart. Kapow! She sure is cute. You have condoms, at least?"

"Of course."

Which is a lie. A few weeks ago, I had to throw my condom supply in the garbage. For one thing, they were all wrecked from lying around at the bottom of my backpack, and two, their expiry date had passed. And it wasn't as if my days had been brimming with opportunities to use them. It mostly felt symbolic.

Seb guesses as much.

"Don't be a dick. Go buy new ones. You don't want to be caught with your pants down in this situation. That would be too stupid."

"Yeah, I will. Yeah, you're right."

Of course he's right. As soon as I can, I run to the pharmacy at a time when I know there won't be too many customers. I don't want to buy them in front of witnesses.

The weekend finally arrives. I have the house all to myself. I've spent the morning cleaning so the place doesn't look like too much of a dump. I check the clock for the hundredth time. Catherine should arrive by bus just after one o'clock. Unless there's a problem and she misses the Number 70, which would make her an hour late. Argh! I cross my fingers. I have no choice but to wait patiently. I stand by the window like a little dog.

Right on schedule, Catherine gets off the bus. She rings the bell.

"Hi!"

That smile, those dimples, that look. Ah! It's worth a million bucks. It's crazy.

"Hi!" I say back, trying to contain my excitement.

I take her coat, hang it in the closet. She keeps a small purse that she slings over her shoulder. I want to kiss her right away, but I hold back. I should give her a hug. Can I put my arms around her? I think so. But in the end I don't, because I should have done that before I took her coat, and now it's just going to look weird.

It's the first time that a girl I'm interested in and who seems to be interested in me has come to my house. I have no idea what to do now. I should have talked to Seb about it. I could give her a tour and end up in the living room. It's a fairly neutral place, which should make us both more relaxed.

"Are you going to show me your room?"

"Uh ... yeah."

It's the smallest room in the house. It's simple, comfortable. There's my desk, a dresser, a few shelves with books, cassettes and a few CDs, and my old captain's bed that's now too small for me. At the foot of it, I've set up the old family TV that I rescued from the basement, but the image only comes on in black and white. A transistor probably burned out.

"Here's my room," I say simply.

Catherine looks at the posters on the walls, the piles of novels. She opens a comic and flips through it without really looking at the drawings. While she browses, I don't move, not sure what I'm supposed to suggest as an activity. I'm trying to organize my thoughts so I don't look like too much of an idiot. Catherine puts down her little purse and turns to me. Something in her look hypnotizes me.

Suddenly my mouth goes dry. She comes closer.

"Would you like to do *something else?*"

She puts her hands around my waist, presses against me, lifts her head up to mine. The message finally makes it to my brain. I take her in my arms, bend my head and go for it ... so to speak. I kiss her. "Kiss" might not be the right word. We make out. For real! We don't stop except to take a breath, then we go back at it.

Catherine steps back, pulls me with her onto the bed. I bury my head in her neck, it tickles her. If her little moans are anything to go by, she likes it. And I was right! She smells like peaches. It's intoxicating.

Lying on top of her like this, I can feel her body beneath mine, her breasts beneath her sweater. Catherine uses her legs to press closer. It's impossible for me to hide the erection that has appeared in my pants, but it doesn't seem to bother her. In fact, she moves her hips, rubs against me.

"Wait," I say. "I'm ... stuck."

My penis has risen in the wrong direction. It's not ideal. I go to move it back, but Catherine grabs my hand.

"Let me."

While looking into my eyes, she smiles. I feel her undoing my pants. Then her hand slips into my boxers. She grabs it, pulls it up and starts to caress me. I close my eyes and dare to slip my hand under her sweater to squeeze her breast. With her free hand, she pulls my head down and presses her mouth to mine.

"Do you want to fuck?"

Her question leaves me speechless. Of course I do. But I hadn't imagined it happening like this. She's just asked me to fuck like she would ask if I wanted some chips.

I must have a weird look on my face, because Catherine takes her hand out of my pants.

"Are you okay?"

"Uh ... yes. It's just that ..."

"You're a virgin?"

"Yeah. You?"

The question just came out like that. It's so not important. Well, okay, maybe a little, actually. A second passes before Catherine answers, a second during which I guess the answer is no. It's reassuring to know she has experience, to know I'm in good hands.

She sits up on the bed.

"Do you want to?"

"Yes ... I think. Yeah, of course. Sorry. It's just that ... woo! Ha!"

I am just a wee bit nervous. Where to begin? Do we keep kissing and touching each other while we're completely dressed, or do we ...

"Do you have condoms? If you don't, I have some," Catherine says, taking charge.

She leans over, grabs her bag and takes out a shiny little package. She throws me the most sensual look I've ever seen and bites her lower lip. I kiss her and ask the question I've been dying to ask ever since I first saw her at the party.

"Do you want to go out with me?"

Her expression changes. The flirty smile disappears. The heat in the room suddenly drops several degrees. Catherine stares at me as if there's been a misunderstanding. She pulls down her sweater.

"Listen, Pierre-Yves, you're cute. I like you, but I don't want a boyfriend right now. What I'm interested in is a one-night stand ... a one-afternoon stand," she jokes. "Okay? You look like your puppy just died."

No, this can't be. In the space of a thousandth of a second, the blood has drained from my body. There is no longer any trace of arousal filling my boxers. The happy feeling that had come over me has evaporated. Worse, I feel sick. Sick like someone has injected acid in my veins.

"I thought ... I thought things really clicked between us."

"Yeah, sure, but ... not like that," Catherine says sympathetically. "I'm sorry. I thought it's what you wanted, too."

Catherine asks me one last time if I want to sleep with her, as if that will fix the problem. But my head and my body are too confused for me to answer. I blame myself. I'm mad at myself for getting carried away, for letting my heart race, for having all those fantasies about her becoming my girlfriend!

It can't be a pretty sight. The girl of my dreams is right beside me in my room, in my bed, she wants to sleep with me, and I am in a semi-catatonic state because I didn't know how to read the signs.

Catherine stays with me and consoles me. Maybe she's feeling empathetic. Maybe she feels sorry for me. I am too stunned to feel ashamed. She tries to change things up, suggests we watch a movie, but nothing works. After a while, she says she's gonna go home. She gives me a little peck on the cheek, says she's sorry for what happened and leaves.

When I recover my senses, the first thing that goes through my head is that I am such a moron, that it's all my fault, that if I hadn't said anything, I would at least have been able to sleep with her but no, I had to open my big fat mouth. What an idiot!

This story about the guy who wanted a girlfriend and the girl who just wanted to fuck should end there. With Seb, who cheers me up while making fun of me the way only a friend knows how to do — "Come on, man! She was right there in your bed!"

And time, the great problem solver, will fix things and eventually let me forget this disaster of a story.

Ha ha! No way! It gets worse. Honest.

During the following weeks, I manage the situation like a pro, which means that one day I feel like staying in bed rolled up in a little ball moping, and the next day I try to convince myself that I should just accept the crumbs Catherine was willing to offer. Except I don't have the courage to call her and ask for sex. I far prefer to wallow in my misery.

It's fucking pathetic. I am suffering like only a teen in love can suffer. A kick in the balls would hurt less. Despite the rejection, despite the pain, my heart remains stuck on her like a fish on a hook.

Damn teenaged stubbornness.

Seb does his job as best friend. He listens to me, he makes me laugh with his stupid jokes, makes sure I don't get too depressed or left alone, tries to get me to change my mind as best he can, but he sees it's not helping.

Sometime in May, he convinces me to give her a call, because prom is coming up. I've bought two tickets and I still haven't asked anyone to go with me.

"Come on, man! You know she's the one you want to invite. Maybe she's realized she made a mistake. Stop jerking off and call her! Worse comes to worst, she'll say no and you'll be able to move on."

"Yeah ... okay," I sigh. "Okay. I'll try."

I hold Catherine's number in my hand. The penciled digits have faded a little from being crushed in my pocket, but they're still legible, and still brimming with the hope from our first meeting.

Seb gives me valuable advice. "First, lose the attitude. If you're depressed, she'll feel it. You need to sound like you've got a smile on your face, man. And don't dwell on what happened too much, okay? It was just a misunderstanding. You're a big boy and you've moved on. Even better, don't talk about it at all! Try to seem a bit disinterested, but not too much. You want her to feel like you want her to say yes, but at the same time, she needs to think you have other fish in the sea, so if she says no, well, it won't be the end of the world."

*

"Hello?"

"Hi, it's me."

"Hello! I'm glad you called."

Again I hear that smile in her voice putting a spell on me. I feel that same excitement. Fuck Sébastien's advice. I forgive Catherine for everything. I put all my eggs in one basket. I'm all in.

"Have you got your CEGEP response?" she asks.

"What? Uh, yeah, I got into Bois-de-Boulogne. Pure science."

"Cool!"

"Yeah. A little gang of us from MSL are going. What about you?"

"I don't graduate until next year," she reminds me, laughing.

"Right."

We make up for lost time by talking about ordinary stuff. She's easy to talk to. It feels good.

So much so, that at one point, I confess, "I think about you a lot."

"Oh yeah?"

I'm standing on the edge of a cliff. I'm just a step away from throwing myself into the abyss. The days of stepping back or hiding from danger are over. If I'm going to fall, so be it. Something in Catherine's voice encourages me, tells me that I am going to take flight.

"Catherine, uh … I wanted to ask if you'd like to go to the graduation prom with me."

A second passes. I hold my breath.

"I would love that."

I would love that. She would love that! My heart instantly explodes with joy.

As soon as I hang up, I call Seb because I am on cloud nine. I rock! Life is beautiful! Life is fucking beautiful, because I am going to finish high school on a high note — as good as the marks on my report card! I need to share this with my best friend.

"Yes! Yes! I knew it!" he shouts, as happy as I am, before launching into a drum solo over the phone.

With work to hand in, studying, final exams and my fantasies about Catherine, the month of June passes like a snap of my fingers. Soon it's June 26th. Through a funny set of circumstances, Seb finds himself going with Annie.

I think that's cool, because the grad prom is a big deal, and we're all going to experience it together. Technically, it's not his grad, but honestly, who cares.

Since Seb's father has agreed to lend him the car, he's going to be our chauffeur. Catherine, who lives on the other end of the island, is going to meet us at my place.

"Nervous?" Seb asks me when he sees me pacing.

"I'm hot. I'm about to sweat right through my shirt."

"Relax, man. You look cute as hell. This is the night you score."

Finding a suit that will, I hope, match Catherine's dress has not been a small matter, especially because my arms are too long, but I think I managed pretty well. My jacket and pants are green linen, which is supposed to breathe better in the warm weather. And the cream-colored shirt goes great with it. It's understated, but a change from black.

A car arrives. When Catherine gets out, the sight of my date takes my breath away. Seb gives me a pat on the shoulder.

"You've hit the jackpot!" he whispers proudly in my ear.

Catherine is wearing a flowered dress in red ocher, which is both disarmingly simple and absolutely fabulous. Her loose hair falls over her shoulders and light makeup highlights her features.

"You look gorgeous," I manage to tell her.

Her cheeks flush. Maybe because of my compliment, maybe because of the heat wave.

After our parents take the required photos, we get into Seb's car to pick up Annie. Then we head for the Château Champlain in downtown Montreal.

The trip is a little quieter than I'd imagined, but I put that down to nervousness. My own mind is otherwise occupied. I imagine Catherine laughing and pulling me into a corner of the room to steal a kiss, which turns into another of our passionate make-out sessions. I think about slow dancing, glued against one another, forgetting everyone around us. I'm already thinking about the end of the evening, taking off her underwear, thinking about her breasts, her naked body ...

If I'd been thinking ahead, I would have booked a room in the hotel and to hell with the after-party!

Hand in hand, we head to the ballroom where the fifth-year Mont-Saint-Louis teachers greet us and offer us a glass of punch. Everyone is dressed up. The girls look chic and the guys are dressed to the nines. High school is finally over, that's something to celebrate.

When Catherine notices that girls from her school are here, too, she runs into their arms and they are so happy you'd think it was their own prom. It's incredibly cute! I go to join them but because I don't really know anyone, I stand back.

"Umm ..."

"You remember Pierre-Yves?" She introduces me as she continues to chat with her friends.

If I'm going to have the slightest chance of making

it work between her and me, I have to try to follow Sébastien's advice. For real, this time. Basically, let her know that I'm attracted to her, but without going overboard. I don't want to look like her lapdog. I want her to want me and jump into my arms. So I make the rounds of the room and greet my friends. We congratulate each other on having made it through the five years. At one point I find Catherine in the middle of another group.

Later, Seb and I are emptying bottles of red and white to create glasses of rosé. I offer one to Catherine, who refuses.

"I'm going to go and say hi to my friends."

"Okay …"

I grab her hand. She smiles at me, lets go and leaves. From the other side of the table, Seb shakes his head.

"Did I miss something?" Annie says when she comes back to the table.

"No, nothing. Here's to the end of your high school!" Seb says, raising a glass of our 1994 special vintage.

We drink, we joke around, and when the DJ starts to play an ABBA song, everyone hits the dance floor.

Catherine hasn't come back. She must still be busy talking, I tell myself. But no. She's over on the other side of the room dancing just like I'd imagined. I feel a small pang in my heart. It must be the wine. After watching her for three songs, I start to tell myself that it sucks to spend my prom without my date. I go to ask her to dance.

"Soon," she answers.

The knockout is brutal. It's only because my brain excels in denial that I manage to stay on my feet. As the evening progresses, it becomes clear that "soon" means never. Catherine is not coming back.

And here I thought that the two of us ...

Argh. A sock left behind the dryer gets more consideration than this. Catherine has just yanked out the arrow that she plunged into my heart when we met. It's going to leave a lasting scar, that's for sure.

I signal to Seb that my evening is over. He already knows. There's nothing to say. He feels bad for me. We'll talk later. I can take the metro home.

Fuck the after-party. Fuck girls. Fuck love.

My virginity and I were doing just fine before this. I didn't need some girl coming and interfering with my life, especially to play with my feelings and take advantage of me. No. I've had enough! I make a firm resolution. This way I can concentrate on what's important. My studies and my novels.

I live just fine with the ridiculous stubbornness of a bruised lover ...

Until a few weeks later, when I meet Marie-Noëlle.

My first.

Acknowledgments

With thanks to sex therapist Laurence Desjardins for the illuminating conversation.

Editor KARINE GLORIEUX teaches literature at the Collège de Maisonneuve in Montreal and is the author of several novels for adults and young people.

SHELLEY TANAKA is an award-winning author, translator and editor who has translated more than forty books for children and young adults. Shelley lives in Kingston, Ontario.